# AMARYLLIS

# AMY
# AMARYLLIS

*Sally Odgers*

📚 Angus&Robertson
An imprint of HarperCollins*Publishers*

*The author wishes to*
*acknowledge the support*
*of the Literature Board*
*of the Australia Council,*
*the federal government's arts*
*advisory and support organisation.*


*AN ANGUS & ROBERTSON BOOK*
*An imprint of HarperCollinsPublishers*

*First published in Australia in 1992 by*
*CollinsAngus&Robertson Publishers Pty Limited (ACN 009 913 517)*
*A division of HarperCollinsPublishers (Australia) Pty Limited*
*25-31 Ryde Road, Pymble NSW 2073, Australia*

*HarperCollinsPublishers (New Zealand) Limited*
*31 View Road, Glenfield, Auckland 10, New Zealand*

*HarperCollinsPublishers Limited*
*77-85 Fulham Palace Road, London W6 8JB, United Kingdom*

*National Library of Australia*
*Cataloguing-in-Publication data:*

*Odgers, Sally Farrell, 1957-*
  *Amy Amaryllis.*

  *ISBN 0 207 17435 0*

  *I. Title.*

*A823.3*

*Cover illustration by Bruce Whatley*
*Typeset by Midland Typesetters, Maryborough*
*Printed in Australia by Griffin Paperbacks*

*5  4  3  2  1*
*96 95 94 93 92*

# 1. AMY

## *Amy*

On the day when she first saw the old green book, Amy Day was bored and unhappy.

The book was lying casually in a cracked and bulgy cardboard carton under a jumble of what her mother called has-beens and never-weres.

The weather was summerish, sticky and hot. Not a day for anything active. More the sort of day for going downtown, hanging about the mall with Caz and the gang . . .

('Stop! Stop!' screamed Amy's mind. 'Don't even think about that!')

It was the fifth day of January, a Monday. Amy didn't want to think about that either. Caz's deadline was eight days away. Sharon had gloatingly reminded her the day after Christmas.

('If you haven't delivered by the 13th, you're out, Day, you're nothing!')

Stop!

At school they all wanted to be in Caz's gang. You couldn't just join: you had to earn your place. Once a member, you left on pain of being declared a nothing. But who would want to leave? It was never dull in Caz's gang. Caz was full of excellent ideas.

Amy had been a member for four months—ever since Caz and her family had moved into Severne Crescent next door to Gran. Suddenly, Amy had six good friends, fellow gangers, pledged to her forever.

Then, on the last day of school, Caz had had her wildest idea yet.

For the first time, Amy had had to say no. She didn't think that this idea of Caz's was so cool. She'd tried to make a joke of it, but it hadn't gone down too well. Caz had been hurt, and Caz had gently delivered her terms. If Amy didn't want to be part of the gang any more, Amy had only to say so.

It wasn't that, Amy had said hastily. She just didn't like the idea. How about doing something else instead?

'You think about it,' said Caz. 'If you want out, just don't turn up on the 13th.'

'Look, I didn't say I wanted out . . .'

'Not now,' said Caz, closing the discussion with a sweep of her hand. Amy had to make up her mind by the 13th. And just to make sure that no-one tried to push her into it, nobody would have anything to do with her until then. And, of course, if she decided she didn't want to stay in the gang, nobody would have anything to do with her ever again.

After Christmas, thinking Caz hadn't meant it, Amy had gone to visit Gran and then gone on to the pool to practise her diving. But Caz was already at the pool and Caz *had* meant it. Amy's new Walkman had somehow ended up in the water.

'Oh, what a pity,' Caz had said. 'What a clumsy thing to do.'

Amy knew that Caz wasn't clumsy.

The day she had ridden her bike to Katie's place, Katie had shut the door in her face. Barbara had done the same thing and Sharon had taken to cruising past Amy's place calling the days off like a night watchman to make sure Amy got the point.

Amy got the point. What Caz said, went, and no-one would be friends with Amy until Amy did her bit.

Amy tried to believe it was only a joke, but underneath she knew it wasn't. Caz and the gang were serious. It was horrible. It was also stupid and boring.

She wandered out onto the porch where her brother Craig was being bored as well. Boredom made Craig bloody-minded.

'Go away, Creepface,' he snarled. He was trying to eat a sandwich, but Reg the dog wanted it too. Craig had to stand on his toes and keep his elbow in the air.

'Geez, Bro, I'm only breathing!' said Amy, injured. 'Or perhaps you've got an exclusive licence on the oxygen round here? Geez, you'd make some money then!' She gave him a quick grin, but Craig was in a snarly mood and wouldn't grin back.

Amy sighed, and fed Reg a bit of cheese. He ate it with a sideways crocodile snap, his gaze never leaving the sandwich in Craig's hand.

Craig dropped him the crust.

'I wish!' he sneered.

'I'm *borrrrred*, and you're *borrrring*,' drawled Amy. She draped her arms and her chin over the porch railing and let her weight hang down. Her eyes rolled, but Craig wasn't going to be amused.

'Listen, El Creepo,' he said. 'You're no orphan. Dad's so bored he's mowing the lawn. Mum's so bored she's spring cleaning. In January! Even Reg is bored now there's no more food to nick. So what's so special about you? Geez, why am I wasting my breath?'

Amy shrugged, nearly strangling herself. 'Let's go swimming,' she suggested, brightening. Surely the gang wouldn't try anything at the pool if Craig was there. And what was the use of having an elder brother if you couldn't make use of him occasionally?

'You must be out of your tree,' said her brother with deep disgust, and he scuffed off next door to see if Todd Foster was bored too. Normally he didn't waste time on Todd, but everyone else had gone away.

Amy grimaced. She loved swimming. It was the only thing she was good at apart from making things up, but she couldn't go to the pool alone.

Craig was the pits. The armpits.

'Amy! Aa-my!' called Jan. 'Come in here!'

Amy unhitched herself from the rail and went in, rubbing at the grooves it had made in her arms and chin. I must look like the bottom of a cake that's been too long on the cooler, she thought. Amycake. With 15+ icing and a cakefrill round the ears.

Jan was pulling cardboard boxes out of the cupboard above the hot water cylinder. Her cotton skirt looked tired and crumpled, and so did Jan. 'Aa-my!' she called again. 'Aaaa-my!'

'I'm here,' growled Amy from behind, forcing her voice down towards her feet. Her mother almost fell off the chair.

'Goodness, Amy,' she complained. 'You scared me out of a year's growth.'

'Outwards?' suggested Amy. 'Geez, you ought to give me a bonus!'

'Chee Kee! Since you're so witty, how about sorting these boxes for me?' said Jan. 'Tip everything out and we'll make three different heaps. One for the tip, one for Vinnie's and one to keep. OK?'

Amy considered. This was slave labour. The sort of thing parents inflicted on bored kids. On the other hand, she had nothing better to do. 'Might as well,' she conceded.

'Don't sound so enthusiastic!' recommended Jan. 'You might find yourself in the saltmines instead.'

That meant tidying her bedroom.

Amy dropped to her knees and clawed at Jan's skirt hem. 'Oh great queen! Anything but that!' she moaned.

'Boxes!' said Jan.

And after all it was quite an interesting job. There were all sorts of things in the boxes. Ancient china animals, dolls with loose legs or missing heads, tatty old postcards.

A cracked and crumbling circlet of artificial flowers caught Amy's attention for a moment. 'Grossissimo!' she said gleefully, putting it on.

Jan made a face. 'I wore that on my head when your

Auntie Sue got married—you know—Jon-the-cop's mum? I was a flowergirl in mauve frills and I thought I was just Christmas.'

'And you've kept it all this time!' Amy was impressed. The thing was so stiff and brittle and horrible.

Jan counted on her fingers. 'Twenty-six and a bit years,' she said briskly. 'Quite long enough. Out it goes. Come on, Amy, it might have silverfish, and next thing you know they'll be chomping into your hair. Oh, look at this lace! Great-Gran made that. It was her own pattern and now no-one knows how to do it. I wish I'd asked her to teach me . . .'

While Amy sorted, Jan pursued dustballs across the top of the cupboard. She kept drifting over and transplanting things from one heap to another, and telling Amy snippets of family history. 'Weird how all this collects,' she mused. 'Most of it's been hanging about for years.' She lifted a very small saucer out of the second pile. 'Most of it's no earthly good.'

'What's that?' asked Amy.

Jan shrugged. 'Who knows?'

'What about this?' Amy dug out a book.

No alarm bells rang, no warning lights flashed. Her fingertips didn't even prickle.

She actually yawned as she brushed off a bit of lint clinging to the subdued green cover.

Jan shrugged again. Jan was a great one for shrugging. 'Just a book I've had for ages.'

Amy opened the book and turned over the pages. They were thick and rich-looking with a narrow gold border looping like a ribbon bow across the top. 'It's blank,' she said. 'What is it? *The Collected Wisdom of Craig Day*?'

Jan snorted. 'Don't you two ever stop?'

'Me—sometimes. Him—never. What's it for?'

'Great-Gran gave it to me when I was your age,' said Jan. 'She said I was to use it for something special.'

'Like donating to Vinnie's?' suggested Amy.

Jan shook her head rather sadly. 'The right thing never came up. I suppose it never will now. Tell you what, Amy, you have it. See if you can make a better job of it than I did.'

Amy stuffed the book down the front of her baggy T-shirt with never a premonitionary tingle. No doubt it would come in handy for something.

It was Mike's turn to cook that evening, but he cheated with cold meat and salad. Amy and Craig washed up in sulky silence while Jan pottered happily in the garden.

The day ended like any other summer day with a shower, an hour of television, a couple of chapters of her library book, and bed. Craig was still feeling ratty. He complained loudly to Jan and Mike that none of his friends ever had to go to bed at ten o'clock.

'It's still flamin' daylight!' he said, loudly injured. 'Flamin'' was as close as he got to swearing at home. Stronger words slipped out quite naturally in the schoolground.

Amy lay blinking at the window, where a pale square of sky still showed. She listened resignedly as the argument waxed, swelled and developed into a full-scale row.

7

Craig thought *he* had troubles. She could have told him a thing or two about troubles, and now, at the end of the day, Caz and the gang came flocking back into her mind.

To shove them away, she began to play her old going-to-sleep game. In it, she was an author, writing the life story of Amy Day.

'There was an ordinary girl called Amy Day,' said Amy inside her head. 'She lived with her mum and dad and horrible brother Craig in a house in a street in a town in a country. She had a dog called Reg and her best friend was called Caz. One year she won the under-fourteen championship at the swimming carnival.'

That was about as far as the story went, because it was a true one.

The younger Amy had gone into all sorts of details about the pool and the other kids at school, but suddenly, lying there watching the sky square getting darker and hearing the mutter of the telly and the escalating fuss in the next room, the older Amy sighed loudly enough to stir the butterfly mobile above her bed.

Things had changed since she last played the game. Caz wasn't her friend at the moment. No-one was.

In her mind, Amy took a big black marker and crossed out Caz's name.

She wished she could cross out Caz.

Of course, if she agreed to do it, Caz would forgive her.

Now Craig was yelling, and soon Mike's patience would snap and he'd stop making reasonable replies and start yelling back. And then Craig would rage off to his room.

As she waited for the explosion from her father, Amy turned her thoughts to the future, beyond the 13th, which would, in Caz's eyes, render her an invisible nothing. But if she *did* do what Caz said, wouldn't that make her into something worse?

What if she had to lie here every night for the rest of her life knowing she was a nothing? Or worse?

It gave her the creeps.

Her back was sweating, so she sat up and wrapped her arms around her bunched-up knees. They were brown bony knees, with a network of fine scratches made by Reg as he leapt off her lap in pursuit of the next-door cat. Minor scratches. What a pity. More 'Sffft' than 'Ouch!', as Jan would say.

Now if only it had been a proper accident, with hospital, plaster and crutches, all her problems would have been solved. For Caz couldn't possibly have expected her to turn up on the 13th then.

A loud and furious whacking sound came from the next room.

There! Mike was laying into the vinyl chair back. When Mike started bashing up the furniture it was time to leave home. It sounded as if the chair had gone right over, but Jan always said she'd rather have battered furniture than battered kids.

'Shut—up—boy!' roared Mike.

'I don't want to hear another word about it,' mouthed Amy, wiggling her eyebrows ferociously.

'I don't want to hear another word about it!' yelled Mike.

'You're going to bed and that's final,' muttered Amy, smiting air.

'You're going to bed and that's final!' howled Mike.

'Yes—*sir*!' said Craig, just this side of insolence. His bedroom door thudded open, and Mike's voice dropped and fizzed out. Jan said something soothing.

Amy could hear Craig's voice now, giving Craig's opinion of Mike in a vindictive whisper. She hoped Mike couldn't hear it too.

What would happen next all depended on Craig. He was quite capable of getting his second wind and going out for another round. But Craig had evidently had enough for one day because his Christmas CD came on with the series of popples and zlits that heralded the beginning of Craig's current favourite, 'Electric Aye'.

One night, thought Amy, hugging her knees, Craig the Blackhearted leapt from his window and galloped into the night with his faithful sister Amyissimo the Golden in hot pursuit . . .

She drummed her hands lightly on her knees, making dramatic music for the Great Escape, but it wasn't much use. Craig the Blackhearted didn't want Amyissimo the Golden along and said so. Loudly.

Amy went back to her autobiography, making changes as she went.

'There was a girl named . . . ' What?'

'Electric aye aye aye, Electric ay-ya! Electric aye yi! yi! Electric ayeee,' sang Craig savagely.

'Hey, Crags,' called Amy softly through the dividing wall.

10

Craig interrupted himself. 'Yeah?' he said unhelpfully.
'What's a name like Amy Day only better?'
'Can't hear you,' sang Craig, two up and one down.
'I thought of Amyissimo, but that's no good.'
'Bury your head,' recommended Craig invisibly. 'I can't be bothered with you, Creepface.'

Wasn't that the truth? Craig couldn't be bothered with anyone.

Amy went back to bed.

Ashley, Alison, Anna, Alicia, Afton, Amaryllis—Amaryllis? She liked that one. It sounded special and it was a little bit like Amy. Yes, Amaryllis. Now who else would she need for her story?

Fifteen minutes later, Amy had it settled. Amaryllis Loveday lived with her brother Crag and her parents the Lady Jasmin and the Lord Michael in a castle in—in—well, in another world. A world without Caz, without Sharon, without malls.

Amaryllis had a faithful hound called Red who protected her from enemies. Red was a special sort of dog. Not one that could talk, but a sort of magical bodyguard. A luck dog? No, that had been done before. A guardhound? Not quite. A spellhound. Trained to detect evil. Yes! She liked that.

Her eyes were sandy with sleepiness, so she lay down again. She was drifting cosily towards a dream when a thought popped into her mind.

What if she forgot the things she'd invented?

Amy stumbled out of bed. There was a pen lying on the floor by her desk, but no paper.

Botherissimo, thought Amy. She was swaying slightly

11

on her feet, which was rather interesting. She must be utterly exhausted.

Sway forwards—pale yellow Footrot Flats nightie and thin bare legs in sight. Sway back. Wallpaper, window and square of sky. Weird.

Feeling seasick, Amy sat down at her desk in a hurry and picked up the green book that Jan had given her.

It had been given for something special, and now she knew what. She would write her story about the beautiful Amaryllis Loveday in a book instead of just planning it in her head.

She wouldn't show it to anyone—except Gran. Yes! She'd send it to Gran when it was finished, and if Gran liked it, she might get it published. Amy Day—Author.

She hoped it would take her a good long time to write it. Preferably the rest of the holidays.

Dizzily, she opened the first gold-edged page and uncapped the initialled pen Gran had given her for Christmas.

\* \* \*

*In a castle on a cliff above the great Sea of Storms in the land of Ankoor lived Amaryllis Loveday. Her father was Lord Michael, a very important person who loved Amaryllis so much that he gave her a priceless namegift: a spellhound named Red. As long as Red was with her, nothing could harm Amaryllis . . . not even Lord Michael's enemies, who were jealous of his wealth and power. At the castle Amaryllis had a very good friend . . .*

\* \* \*

Amy yawned, and laid down the pen. She closed the green book, and rocked her way back to bed.

She really was incredibly tired, but now she had something to look forward to. Something she could do alone, without any help from Craig or Caz and the gang.

Suddenly, she could hardly wait for the morning.

## 2. AMARYLLIS

# *Amaryllis*

n the day that she first saw the old green ledger, Amaryllis Loveday was bored and unhappy. A sullen summer storm was grumbling around the craglands and she had been unable to leave the castle in three days.

Amaryllis sighed. Three days spent in the austere company of her lady mother. As many as three more to follow? Oh, impossible!

As usual Lady Jasmin had made sure her daughter had no opportunity to visit the reinbeast on the craglands, nor even to discuss estate matters with the steward. Why, thought Amaryllis rebelliously, could she not have been a son? As a daughter she was kept close in the castle. Her only regular contact with the reinbeast she loved was when she wore their fleece.

Life was much more bearable when Lord Michael was home, but he and Amaryllis' brother Crag had ridden off to Western Port two days before. Silent

Thomas had gone with them and even Master Greenhaven the tutor had deserted his post to attend his
father's sickbed in the north.

She much preferred Master Greenhaven's lessons to
her mother's efforts to turn her into a lady.

'A daughter of the Nine Castles does not concern
herself with such.' That was Lady Jasmin's stock reply
to most of Amaryllis' requests.

Why had she had to be born of the Nine Castles
anyway? Looped about by traditions and expectations,
guarded through every portion of the day, having to act
in accordance with her position, not her heart. And if
she must be a victim of traditions, why must it be those
of the hidebound Fourth and Fifth Castles? Though even
they were better than the dark mysteries which attended
the Seventh.

Amaryllis shivered, and her hand rose automatically
to her birthchain to ward off the thought of those strange
wanderers of the Seventh Castle.

Tapestry and deportment, running households and
guarding one's tongue: there must be more to life than
that, and she knew there *was* more. Master Greenhaven
had taught Amaryllis Loveday more than her letters and
numberlore, and *how* Lady Jasmin would have scolded
had she known! Master Greenhaven had taught her to
question. To Lady Jasmin's mind, questions smacked of
the renegades who ridiculed the established order, yet
still had the impudence to style themselves the 'Tenth
Castle'.

A cool muzzle thrust against her hand, and Amaryllis
looked down at her companion. 'Oh, Red!' she sighed.

'Here is a question. Why is everything *so* . . . ?'

The spellhound nudged at her hand and whined, noiselessly shifting his paws. His function was to guard Amaryllis, not to love her, and yet he somehow managed to do both. Had Lady Jasmin suspected, she would have considered this a grave flaw. A spellhound's business was to be coldly singleminded.

'Other people have adventures,' said Amaryllis. 'Even Sophie, and she a tower maid! She came from the east, Red, across the mountains and desert, so she must have had adventures on the way. But she'll not tell me more than a whisper, for fear Lady Mother will scold.'

Red waved his plumy tail and the air prickled. 'An idea indeed!' said Amaryllis. 'We shall go to the tower and talk to Sophie and be bored no more.'

She rose carefully to her feet, lifted her long skirts clear of the floor, ducked through the tapestry screen and set off up the narrow staircase that spiralled to the top of the tower. This servants' stair allowed Amaryllis to pass about the castle unseen. Not that she had reason to hide and spy, but it was fitfully entertaining—unlike conversing with Crag.

Amaryllis pulled a sour face. Fortunate Crag, gone with Lord Michael to Western Port. Crag hated riding and hated the cares of the castle estate. He wished only to be a minstrel, but Lady Jasmin would hear nothing of that. A son of the Nine Castles was destined to follow his lord father.

Amaryllis had begged to go to Western Port as well, but Lady Jasmin had said gravely that she had not earned the privilege, and so all Lord Michael could do was shake his head. Perhaps next time, if it pleased Lady Jasmin.

Amaryllis did not find this encouraging.

She had scarcely rounded the first spiral when she heard her lady mother's voice.

'Amaryllis! Amaryllis!'

Amaryllis froze on the stair, one hand on the smooth stone railing. Would Lady Jasmin go away?

'Amaryllis!'

Lady Jasmin was coming closer. Amaryllis could hear the click of her slipper heels on the floor. She sighed and slipped back down the stairs. When her mother entered the round bed chamber the girl was seated calmly in her high-backed chair.

'Amaryllis! Why did you not answer me?' Lady Jasmin's voice was cold and her eyes twin chips of crystal.

'I beg pardon, Lady Mother,' said Amaryllis colourlessly. 'I was reflecting.'

'Reflecting! Is that all the girl can do?' demanded Lady Jasmin of the wall.

The wall made no answer.

'Upon my position as a daughter of the Fourth Castle,' said Amaryllis.

'A fitting subject, but be sure your pride is not vainglory,' said Lady Jasmin. 'Since you have no task today, you may come to the coffer attic with me. It is time to make our bundles for the village. Come!' She swished out of Amaryllis' room and swept up the grand central stair, whose pitch was so shallow that it had three times the number of steps of the servants' spiral.

Amaryllis followed, sighing softly.

'Amaryllis!' Sometimes it seemed that Lady Jasmin had eyes in the back of her head. 'How often have I bid you not to lift your skirts like a tower maid?'

Such a question required no answer. 'Your pardon, Lady Mother,' said Amaryllis, letting her skirts fall.

The coffer attic was at the top of the tower. Lady Jasmin swept in like a seaswan. Amaryllis, following, tried not to pant.

'Amaryllis! You are not a reinbeast. Contain your breathing. Your breathing, Amaryllis!'

Oh, if I *were* a reinbeast! thought Amaryllis wistfully. If I were only someone else. The spellhound uttered a warning whine, but Amaryllis heard only her own disobedient breath.

Naturally, it wasn't Lady Jasmin herself who sorted the coffers in the attic. That task was for Sophie and Gillie, the tower maids, who covered their hair with white kerchiefs and masked their skirts with aprons against the dust.

Amaryllis watched impatiently as they dragged metal-studded coffers away from the walls and heaved off the great domed lids. It was they also who lifted out the contents and inhaled the dust and aromatic preservatives of which the coffers reeked. Amaryllis sighed with envy. Her clasped hands itched to touch the bolts of reinbeast weave.

She hated standing idle while others did interesting things. If only her mother would go away. Then she would help Sophie and Gillie. Lord Michael never objected to her friendship with the tower maids.

'Not that.' Lady Jasmin waved an aristocratic hand

at a bolt of glinting blue cloth, woven from the fleece of the prime blue reinbeast. 'That will make up nicely for your new winter mantle, Amaryllis. I feel it should be more richly trimmed this year, and will make an excellent test-piece for my new sewing dame. I pray your lord father has chosen an experienced woman, and has not forgot my other commissions at the port.'

Amaryllis wrinkled her nose. A new mantle. She knew what that meant. Hours of standing in her shift, draped with the soft blue cloth as the sewing dame muttered and pinned and tucked about her. She was bound to mutter and tuck: sewing dames always did. How much more Amaryllis would have enjoyed such a garment had she been permitted to tend the beasts which provided the fleece! She sighed.

The reinbeasts which roamed the craglands were the emblem of the Fourth Castle. Nowhere else did they thrive so well and grow such lustrous fleece. And the animals themselves were so beautiiful, so joyous. Ama- ryllis loved them for themselves as well as the traditions they represented.

'I shall apply to my kinsmen for stargems,' said Lady Jasmin, her thoughts on the mantle.

Stargems! Amaryllis' eyes rounded with surprise. Of course she wore stargems on her birthchain: they were the traditional emblem of Lady Jasmin's family castle. But to wear the costly stones on a mantle as well: that was luxury! It was also one more link in the bonds that held her.

Sophie caught her eye and smiled, delighted with her friend's good fortune.

The coffer was empty. 'These for the bundles,' decided Lady Jasmin, indicating bolts of cloth. 'The softer blue for the new babe at North Cragland . . . yes, Jem?'

A page had panted into the attic. 'Guests, my Lady! Of the Fifth Castle, come out of the south. Hollies is rolling the gates.'

'I shall come.' Lady Jasmin had been born of the Fifth Castle, and her kin held rights over the stargem mines. 'Girls—continue. Miss Amaryllis may oversee the bundles.'

Lady Jasmin departed with a glint of crimson skirts and Amaryllis sprang to drag out another coffer, choosing one from the darkest corner. Cobwebs stretched and broke as the chest came away from the wall. Spiders scurried in panic.

'I doubt it's been opened for a generation,' said Amaryllis with approval. 'What is it, Sophie?'

'Miss . . . The spellhound is alert!' said the maid, drawing back. 'I fear . . .'

Amaryllis glanced at Red. 'Should I not?' she asked, but the hound's deep eyes were unreadable. 'Perhaps there may be reinbeast weave in one of the lost shades!' she said hopefully. 'My lord father hopes one day to breed such shades again. He hopes that the matching of high-sheen beasts may bring the true rose once more. Or even the gold.'

The tower maids nodded agreeably, and Amaryllis sighed. They were her true friends, yet she could expect no enthusiasm from them in this. Bending, she pried up the stiff latch and lifted the lid.

Sophie sneezed. 'Oh, Miss, we were to take the chests

from t'other row first. Oh, Miss, we ought not . . .' Her doubts faded as she took note of the contents of the chest. 'Oh, Miss!' she said in a new tone.

The contents of the coffer were old, old cloths of faded cherry and rose. Some bolts retained the natural singing blue of the reinbeast, shading to green and gold as they caught the light. Amaryllis touched them reverently.

They were soft and lovely, but more than that. Now she understood Red's reaction, for here lay her heritage.

Here would also have lain her future, had she been a son.

And the chest offered other treasures. The unknown grandam who had packed it had had a fancy for lovely things, for she had laid by strange and colourful shells, feathers, soapstone birds and hounds and brittle wreaths of flowers. A flowered girdle of delicate lilac almost crumbled as Amaryllis touched it. 'Ahh,' breathed the tower maids.

'We'll not take of this, Miss?' ventured Sophie.

Amaryllis scrabbled deeper, barely noting a familiar grumble of stone on stone from far beneath. The spellhound grumbled too, so low that Amaryllis felt the sound through her bones. 'Oh, hush, Red,' she said absently. 'It is only Hollies rolling the gates.'

Her fingertips had touched something angular, and she drew out a ledger, bound in green leather, tooled in gold. A name looped across the top of the cover: her name, which she shared with many long-dead kinswomen.

'Ahh,' breathed Amaryllis, echoing the tower maids. She scarcely saw Sophie's hand start to her own birthchain: a modest affair of shell an stone. Sophie, it seemed, distrusted hidden ledgers, particularly in the unchancy green of the Seventh Castle. So perhaps did Red, but though Amaryllis felt the invisible force of his alertness, he made no attempt at prevention.

Later, she wondered at that.

She opened the filigree clasp and scanned the fine pages, but to her disappointment all were blank. That other Amaryllis had left no message. Nevertheless, Amaryllis slid the ledger inside her bodice, tightening her girdle to hold it in place. Perhaps it would bring good fortune—but was that a step on the stair?

When the Lady Jasmin returned, the tower maids were harmlessly sorting bolts of cloth while Amaryllis sat gracefully by with her hands in her lap and the spellhound at her side. Lady Jasmin looked kindly on her daughter.

The evening was spent more tiresomely than usual, for the visiting kinsmen proved grey faced and grey headed and, thought Amaryllis sourly, of grey disposition. The stargems at their collars and girdles winked like embers. Kinsmen or not, she felt no answering spark of interest or affection.

The greyest of all made a fatuous remark about reinbeast. Amaryllis itched to contradict, but continued to sit sedately on her low chair, fingers busy with stitching, mind busy with rebellion.

'Ill news from the west,' sighed one, nibbling at a piece of the cook maid's best art. 'Insurrection is brewing.'

He seemed to enjoy the word and said it again, with full attention to the rolling Rs. 'Insurrection.'

'Indeed.' Lady Jasmin was not much interested in politics, but Amaryllis pricked up her ears.

'The rabble lordlings of the west—Random chief among them—bay in the circle for dividend in the wealth of the Nine Castles. No matter that we and ours have brought our concerns from naught . . . now they wish to take of it for themselves.'

'Reprehensible,' agreed Lady Jasmin.

'A share in the stargem mines, no less!' huffed the grey one. 'Such is their demand! What of your husband, Cousin? Is he not concerned with these creatures of the Tenth Castle? Tenth Hovel, more like.'

'My Lord will no doubt do what is proper,' said Lady Jasmin repressively.

The grey one grumbled on at some length and Amaryllis lost interest. What had rabble lords to do with her? Their forebears must once have had the chance to cultivate the reinbeast. They had failed. The Fourth Castle had succeeded. The story ended there.

When at last Lady Jasmin dismissed Amaryllis, she went thankfully away to the bedchamber, with Red in faithful attendance.

Sophie came to braid her hair, but Amaryllis was worn out with civility and not inclined to talk. Instead, she stroked Red's rich fur and it was like warming her hands at the kindly hearth of his approval.

After Sophie had gone, she rummaged in her chest. Out from its nest in a snowbank of shifts came the green ledger, and out from a high corner shelf came ink and a carved pen.

Amaryllis seated herself and allowed her hand to rest

a moment on the spellhound's head. Then she began to write in the swift curving script taught her by Master Greenhaven. She wrote not of herself and her dreary existence, but of a girl with a short and simple name— like her own and yet not.

\* \* \*

*Amy Day lived in a small dwelling beside a great thoroughfare. Her family was a simple one, not of the Nine Castles, yet respected. Amy was not obliged to learn stitching, and nor did she require constant attendance for her safety. Her spellhound thus was able to attend on whom he pleased, and her own life was of a marvellous freedom. Her lord father Mike had use of a conveyance that could travel untiringly and her lady mother Jan cared not for deportment . . .*

\* \* \*

# 3. AMY
## *Tower*

my hitched her pillow half over her head. What was that appalling noise? It sounded like a dozen stalled bulldozers dragging across a concrete floor.

The ghastly sound ended with a hollow crump, and Amy muttered and relaxed. She'd been dreaming. Or maybe Craig had been revenging himself on Mike by rearranging his furniture in the middle of the night.

Unless a Boeing 747 had crashed into the house?

Amy burrowed. Whatever it was, it could wait until tomorrow.

The next time she woke, the sun was shining directly into her face. She humped over in protest.

Something was wrong.

Amy stared uncomprehendingly at the wall. It was curved. And someone seemed to have replaced her wattle-blossom wallpaper with an arty grey stone pattern. Ridiculous. She was dreaming.

Dreaming she'd woken up and found different wall-paper. Weirdissimo. She turned over. The sunlight was streaming through the window—from the wrong angle. And the window itself was a narrow slit surrounded by more of the grey stone wallpaper.

If it was wallpaper.

Amy found herself sitting upright, gasping and uttering bleats of terror.

This wasn't *her* room.

She'd been kidnapped, that's what. Some lunatic had climbed in her window, held a chloroform pad over her nose, bundled her helpless form into a van with blacked-out windows and fake numberplates and brought her here in the night. And if she made a sound . . .

Amy quaked. If she closed her eyes she'd wake in her own room. Please, God . . . She grasped for the little silver cross she always wore. It had been a present from Great-Gran the Christmas before she died.

But even that had changed. Squinting downwards, Amy saw a string of fiery stones. And where was her Footrot Flats nightie? In place of the manic stare of The Dog was a cluster of embroidered flowers. Loops of gold and blue ribbon festooned the front and, most peculiar of all, draped over each shoulder was a long plait, the colour of lemon butter.

Had someone put her in fancy-dress and a wig for a joke?

Craaazy. Amy tugged experimentally at one of the plaits and her eyes watered. Some joke.

It was no wig. The lemon-butter plait was firmly rooted in Amy's scalp.

The sunlight vanished and blotches danced in front of her eyes. I'm blacking out! thought Amy.

The room swooped around her like the showground when Caz had dared her to ride on the Octopus. She'd been sick afterwards. Like the showground, the room steadied, settled and became still, leaving Amy's insides as a still-whirling centre of the universe.

She found that she was crouched in a vast billow of bedclothes like a mouse in a heap of cotton wool. She tugged at the other plait. Yes, it belonged to her. But—and this, as Jan would have said, was the sixty-four dollar question—who was 'she'?

Because Amy Day had short sunbleached hair in a feathery cut that only just covered her earlobes.

Amy clambered down and scooted across a floor which struck stone-cold at the soles of her feet. A large metal disk was hanging on the wall—not the best of mirrors, but it would do.

Bunching the trailing gown in one hand she peered at her reflection. A little of her panic eased as she recognised her own grey eyes in the dull silvery depths. She touched her face. Hers.

She was still herself, even if her hair would have looked more at home on Rapunzel or a Barbie doll.

She shuffled to the window. It was so narrow and the walls were so thick that she could see only a small wedge of view.

Mountains, and an angry-looking sea.

Crags, dark twisty trees and a few patches of greyish-green.

It wasn't comforting, so Amy climbed back into

bed. Resolutely, she closed her eyes.

She was so frightened she could hear her heartbeats pounding through her body, hear the sigh of breath in her throat. There seemed to be an extra tingle in the air, like the feeling of dipping a finger in a glass of lemonade. She lay until she could bear it no longer. It was either open her eyes or scream.

Someone was looking back at her. The eyes were toffee brown, and framed by long ears the colour of varnish. A dog.

'Reg,' she breathed. 'Reg?'

Of course it wasn't Reg. It wasn't even very like him. Reg was a ragtag dog, mostly setter, all flopping ears and wagging tail and crocodile teeth. This was a rangy, graceful animal, with a coat that shone with grooming, and grave eyes. The dog's gaze held hers and she had the unnerving feeling that it would see right through her and scent her fear.

'Sit down then, good boy,' said Amy, cringing.

The dog sank down obediently. It watched her. Amy stared back, trying not to see the faint tremble in the air which could only be caused by standing tears.

But there was no point in playing possum under the sheets. She slithered to the floor, stumbling over the hem of her nightgown as she tried to avoid the dog. A ribbon loop caught under her foot and tore.

'Blastissimo!' said Amy ferociously, then spun round with a gasp as a tapestry curtain swung aside to admit the face of a pale girl a bit older than Amy. 'Miss?' hissed the girl.

Amy stared. Was this girl part of the gang? A dangling

plait swung into view and she gulped. The kidnap idea was a washout. A kidnapper could have dressed her in a nightie and shut her in a weird room, but no kidnapper on Earth could have caused Amy Day to sprout long lemon-butter plaits in a single night. No kidnapper on Earth . . . Her scalp prickled. UFOs?

'I've come to braid your hair,' said the girl softly. 'If you'd not wish a scold from your lady mother you must be in the Great Chamber soon.'

Amy tried to say something—anything—but her throat seemed to have closed off.

'Please, Miss,' said the girl reproachfully. 'There'll be a great scold for me if you are not ready betimes.'

She spoke with an unfamiliar accent, and her voice was low and sweet. Amy stared at her cropped hair, her strange blue cap and her blue and white scalloped dress, looped up at the front to display a pair of trim ankles and soft leather shoes. She'd never seen anyone who looked like that before. Was she Dutch? Latvian? Martian?

'Your hair, Miss, and quickly.' Dazedly, Amy sat on a high carved stool while the girl unfastened a velvet ribbon from one of the gleaming plaits and began to untwist the strands. Amy wriggled in her seat. She hated having her hair touched, which was why she always wore it short.

The red dog was still staring and everything was impossible, but those busy fingers . . . brrr! To take her mind off them, she unravelled the other plait and was diverted for a moment by the sheer luxurious length of her hair. Undone, it flowed over her shoulders, down the ridiculous nightgown and hung in a waterfall over the back of the stool. Incredible. Fairytale princess stuff.

The dog stared.

Amy shook herself and her voice returned. 'Why does he *do* that?' she asked peevishly.

'The spellhound?' The girl looked astonished. 'Why, 'tis his role, Miss, to be ever watchful.'

A guard dog? Amy swallowed, not liking the sound of that. She had to find out where she was, and quickly. This girl seemed friendly. Could she help? Would she?

'Excuse me,' said Amy cautiously, 'but where are we?'

The girl laughed indulgently. 'Now, Miss, I see what you are at! But indeed there's no time for suppose games now. Your lady mother waits.'

She put down the brush and began to weave an elaborate braid, with a different coloured ribbon in each strand.

'But—who am I?' asked Amy. 'Please?'

'Miss,' said the girl reproachfully.

'My name can't be "Miss",' snapped Amy. If this was a nightmare, politeness hardly mattered.

The girl thought otherwise. 'I beg your pardon, Miss Amaryllis, but Lady Jasmin will be waiting . . . Are you all right, Miss?' she added with alarm for, with a strange gulping noise, Amy had nearly toppled off her stool.

'*What* did you say?' she asked hoarsely.

'Your lady mother will be waiting,' said the girl patiently.

'No—my name—Ama . . .' Amy swallowed, and the words seemed to stick in her throat. 'Is my name Amaryllis Loveday?'

30

'Miss, have you a fever?' The girl's voice was low and concerned.

'No,' said Amy, dry-mouthed. 'But—oh, you don't understand. What am I going to do?' Her voice cracked, and she laughed hysterically. 'I'm still asleep, aren't I? Dreaming?'

'No, Miss, you're truly awake, for all you seem not yourself,' soothed the girl.

Amy seized on this. 'Do I? Look, er—miss—oh, what can I call you?'

'' tis Sophie,' said the girl nervously. 'You know Sophie. And if this is some supposing game, I warn you, Miss, 'twill end in dismissal for me and tears for you.'

'It's no game, Sophie,' said Amy earnestly. 'I only wish it was. I s'pose it's a dream, really. Did you say my name was Amaryllis Loveday and my—my mother is Lady Jasmin? Or am I mixed up?'

Sophie nodded, her hands twisting together unhappily. 'That is your name.'

'And—how long have you known me?' asked Amy.

'For five seasons, Miss, since I came,' said Sophie slowly. 'But what has happened? You have no fever, the spellhound is unalarmed . . .' She glanced down at the dog and back at Amy again. 'Yet somehow you seem not . . .'

'Myself?' said Amy hollowly. 'Greatissimo. Well I'm not myself. Not the self *you* know. Listen, Sophie, my name is Amy, Amy Day, and when I went to sleep last night I was at home in my own bed. Then I heard a noise in the dark . . .'

Sophie nodded. ''twould be the gates,' she said. 'Opening at Lord Michael's command before sunrise.'

'Oh,' said Amy flatly. 'You mean I was here then, and never even noticed?'

A chill walked up her back and she shuddered violently. So she had slept and woken and slept and woken again . . .

'Come.' Sophie unhooked a dress and held it out to Amy. Then she lifted the lid of a wooden chest, put aside a book and began to take out piles of white cloth.

'I woke up and I had long hair and this gross nightie on,' said Amy, and suddenly she could hardly keep from chattering. 'I haven't got to wear all those, have I? I don't know how . . .'

Sophie offered a shift. Amy turned her back, hauled off the nightdress and dived into the white folds. The thing came almost to her ankles. Next came strange loose pants with ties instead of elastic, then another heavier petticoat that fastened at the waist. Thick white stockings hooked to the legs of the pants and pulled uncomfortably as she moved.

Amy looked helplessly at the dress. It was much too long.

Still silently, Sophie dropped the dress over her head and began to fasten a row of tiny buttons that reached from the collar to below Amy's waist. The cuffs were buttoned too. The dress seemed amazingly light and soft, and at any other time Amy would have been enchanted by the shifting shades of blue. But now . . . Sophie produced thin soft leather shoes, more like gloves or moccasins, and watched doubtfully as she fumbled with the fastenings. 'You don't know, do you?' she said wonderingly. 'You truly don't . . . you're witched, and perhaps the spellhound too, just as you've always feared. Oh, Miss!'

Amy looked unhappily back. 'It's no use meeting this Lady Jasmin, is it?' she said. 'She'll know.'

'Miss, never say so,' said Sophie earnestly. 'Go to her now, and never say such a thing to her. Play a part.'

'But she might help!' exclaimed Amy.

Sophie shook her head decidedly. 'Say nothing to Lady Jasmin, but "Yes, my Lady Mother," and "If it pleases my Lady Mother," then come as soon as may be to the tower. Gillie and me—we'll search our minds together and think what's best to be done. Now go.'

'Go where?' asked Amy. 'Is this really a castle?'

'No time now!' cried Sophie. 'Through the next chamber and down the broad stair, Miss, that's the way.'

'But how can I find you?'

Sophie tweaked the hanging tapestry. 'Climb the servants' spiral, straight to the tower,' she said. 'Go, Miss, and quick. You're witched indeed, but Gillie and me, we'll think of something. And keep the spellhound close—he may have virtue yet.' She darted away.

Amy stood helplessly in the middle of the round stone bedroom. She didn't believe it. But, as she moved, the heavy braid of hair swung against her back.

It had to be a dream—or Candid Camera? There was an idea! •

Well, she'd always wanted to be a TV star! So if millions of viewers *were* gawking at her, she might as well give them their money's worth!

'Geronimo!' said Amy, lifting her chin. She gathered her skirts, and stepped onto the landing of a wide flight of stairs.

# 4. AMARYLLIS
## Fever Sheet

maryllis woke in darkness, but she knew immediately that something was wrong. There was a
strange, fresh scent in the air, a green scent, quite
unlike the usual blend of stone-salt-wool that was a
familiar part of her chamber in the tower. She inhaled
deeply.

Could the cook maid have spilt a box of spices? She
frowned in the darkness, wondering what it could be.
Something tangy and delicious . . . What was that? A
regular thudding beat, with a strange wild music behind
it, muffled but disturbing.

Could Crag have returned to the castle with some
uncouth musician from Western Port?

Amaryllis swung her legs out of bed. Her toes cringed
automatically away from the cold floor, but the floor did
not seem to be cold. She leaned down to investigate. Her
exploring hand touched the floor. Carpet?

Amaryllis considered.

Only Lady Jasmin's own apartment had carpet, therefore this could not be Amaryllis' chamber. But how had she been moved to Lady Jasmin's domain while she slept, and why?

As Amaryllis' eyes became accustomed to the darkness, she began to see looming shapes.

One large pale-coloured square in the wall puzzled her immensely. Had her mother worked a new tapestry? She wondered what the design would be: something solemn and uplifting, she was sure. The Lady Jasmin never wasted her time on frivolous scenes.

And what *was* that noise? If a minstrel had come during the night and this was a sample of his art, he would surely be dismissed at daybreak.

Amaryllis' thoughts were broken by the sudden realisation that the tapestry on the wall was growing lighter. The thrumming sound paused, then began again, more softly. Amaryllis put up her hand to push away her braids so that she might hear more clearly.

Then she forgot the mysterious minstrel as cold horror swept in like a mist from the sea.

Her braids were gone!

Wildly, Amaryllis swept her hands over her head, but it was true, horribly true. Her hair had been cut short, cropped like a tower maid's or a fever victim's. She gave a soundless cry, and fell back, grasping for her birth-chain, quite lightheaded.

And no wonder, for if her hair had been shorn there was no doubt that she was very ill indeed with a fever; nothing short of imminent death would have persuaded the Lady Jasmin to sacrifice her daughter's long and shining hair.

Desolate tears swept across Amaryllis' eyes like the incoming tide. The light tapestry was explained now, and so was the pungent scent. The fever sheet had been soaked and wrung in steaming water, and medicinal herbs had been strewn to combat the infection. How long had it been since she lay down to sleep in her chamber? How long since delirium had overtaken her? Would the reinbeast weave selected for her winter mantle form her shroud instead? Her hand groped again for the reassurance of her birthchain; the stargems she had worn since her Naming had proclaimed her a daughter of the Fourth Family and the Fifth.

The chain was there and she grasped it thankfully, but the shape was wrong, the chain was too long and too fine. It felt as if it would snap, and then it did snap and Amaryllis gasped back a scream, half convinced that it spelt her death.

Close by, a strange wailing voice began to chant tunelessly. 'Electric aye aye aye, Electric ay-ya! Electric aye yi! yi! Electric ayeee.'

Amaryllis trembled. Was she dead indeed, that they were singing her dirge? How could she be dead when she could still hear? Perhaps this was no dirge, but a mazing charm. But where was Red? Why was he not here? He should have howled a warning long since.

There was a fierce and sudden pounding on the wall, and the chanting voice and the regular thrumming died away. A low and angry muttering took its place. 'A bloke can't flamin' well do any flamin' thing in this flamin' house!' said the voice viciously.

There was silence for a while, then, quietly, slyly, the thrumming began again, so low that Amaryllis could hear it through the bones of her skull rather than her ears.

And the pale fever sheet glimmered in the growing light.

Amaryllis' skin crawled with sweat, and her eyes kept blurring over. She knew she must not leave her bed: if this were a fever, chill would bring certain death.

Oh, where was Red? She could never remember waking without him before. Even if she could not see him, she should have been aware of his electric presence. But this chamber—this place—was empty of any life but her own. Amaryllis moaned. She wanted Sophie. Even Crag. Anyone to reassure her that she had not been left alone with a strange dirge-singer to die.

She gave up to despair.

A voice broke into Amaryllis' nightmare. 'Come on, sleepy head, if you want any breakfast.'

She opened her eyes unwillingly.

A woman was standing by her bedside.

At least, Amaryllis supposed it was a woman, but what female would wear such garments? A skimpy shift covered her top parts, and her legs were bare beneath blue drawers.

She wasn't wearing stockings, and her hair was cropped short about her head. Amaryllis touched her own hair hopefully, but it still felt short and ragged. Something hurt her palm, and a swift inspection showed the birthchain, broken and crumpled in her hand. But it wasn't *her* birthchain.

'Better get up now, Amy,' said the woman cheerfully. 'Dad's doing the washing and he wants the sheets.'

Amaryllis lay there, staring. The woman looked oddly familiar, but that often happened in dreams.

'OK, Amy love?' said the woman. 'What's the matter? Oh, you've broken your chain. Well that's easily mended. I'll drop it at the jeweller's later on.'

Amaryllis said nothing.

The woman took the birthchain and dropped it into a pouch in her shift. 'You can do your room after breakfast,' she said briskly. 'Come on. Up.' With a swift jerk of her wrist, she peeled the coverlet off the bed. Amaryllis stared down at her sketchy shift in horror. On the front was a design featuring a horrible wild-eyed animal, like nothing she had ever imagined. She gave a low wail of despair.

She was mad, crazed or witched, and she had been shorn and put with other afflicted. Deprived even of Red.

'Don't be silly, Amy,' said the woman quite sharply. 'I've laid your clothes out. Hurry.' She left the chamber.

Cowering, Amaryllis looked about.

The walls were angled and covered all over with a perfectly executed tapestry design of flowers and leaves. The floor was covered with carpet, and in place of her coffer was a low chest with drawers in the sides. On top was a small pile of garments. Another chest bore ledgers.

What she had taken for a fever sheet was a huge square window.

Cautiously, Amaryllis crept over to it. One side was covered with woven metal mesh, but she bumped her head painfully on the other: it seemed to have an invisible wall. Glass, but in what large sheets!

Amaryllis rubbed her head. She touched her face then, but it seemed the same face she'd always had. Timidly, she moved to peer out at greener grass than she had ever seen, a white barricade and a strange yellow building beyond.

A spray of water leapt suddenly from the grass. Her heart gave a glad bound of recognition as a copper-coloured hound trotted across the open space in front of it. The spellhound. She was not unprotected in this strange place!

'Red!' she cried. 'To me!' The animal turned at her voice, and she saw that it wasn't Red at all. A chance resemblance—it was a common animal, no more.

'Amy! Hurry *up*!' called a voice.

Amy. The woman called her Amy. How curious. That was the name she had invented for the minstrel's tale she had begun to write in the green ledger from the coffer room!

Amaryllis sagged with relief. It *was* a dream. This was the proof. She had fallen asleep while weaving her tale and her dreams had carried her into a chronicle of her own imagination.

She would surely wake in good time, but meanwhile she must dream this dream to the end. How big Sophie's eyes would be when she told it!

But before she could regale Sophie with the tale she must wake. And she had no intention of waking until she had savoured this strange experience.

'Onward,' she told herself aloud, and lifted the strange and skimpy garments from the chest.

They were impossible.

Amaryllis put the brief shift on three times, but she could find no fastenings and it didn't fit well. It left her arms bare, which was a peculiar thing indeed. The drawers were worse. If she hadn't seen the woman wearing a similar pair she would have been sure there was some mistake.

She had one more unpleasant shock before she left the chamber. Seeing what she thought was another, smaller window in the wall behind the bed, she moved across to see if the Sea of Storms were here in her dream.

Instead, she saw a pale, pointed face with raggedly cropped hair and grey eyes which regarded her in amazement.

It was only when she put out a shaking hand to indicate friendship that she realised that the thing was a looking glass. Amaryllis peered at her own face, seeing it clearly for the first time. Or *was* it her own? It felt the same, but without her long familiar braids who could be sure?

A tall thin boy slouched into the room, kicking the door open so violently that it bounced off the jamb.

'Crag!' she cried with delight.

For the boy was her brother Crag, altered as she was altered, but unmistakably himself.

'Crag yourself, El Creepo,' said the boy. 'Hurry up. Mum's doing her 'nana and Dad's even worse. He can't've got over last night yet. Geez, I dunno. The flamin' place is a flamin' madhouse. And what's wrong with you? See yourself in the mirror and get a shock?'

Amaryllis was silent. This wasn't Crag after all. It was

as like to him as a twin, but it was no more her own brother than the ragamuffin dog had been Red.

The dream had tricked her again.

The boy who looked like her brother was surprised. 'What's up? Cat got your tongue?'

Amaryllis didn't like the sound of that, but she followed him into a chamber which had wide sunny windows and such gleaming appointments that she closed her eyes, dazzled. The woman was perched on a high padded stool eating something from a gleaming bowl. 'Get yourself some breakfast, Amy,' she said.

Amaryllis blinked. This dream was strange indeed! The boy who looked like Crag gave her a shove between the shoulderblades. 'Wake up, Creepface.'

'No need for that, Craig,' reproved the woman.

The boy rolled his eyes. 'Sorry, El Creepo,' he said elaborately, then pushed past her and began to rattle around, preparing himself a meal.

Amaryllis watched closely. Flakes of what looked like dead leaves in a box turned out to be some sort of milled grain, apparently to be eaten with milk. At least, she supposed it was milk, although it too came out of a box.

Carefully, she began to imitate the boy's actions.

The box of grains was so much lighter than she expected that a shower of the stuff poured over the edges of the eating vessel and flowed down over the strangely patterned table.

'*Amy.*' The woman shook her head.

The milk was easier to handle, but the plain metal spoon seemed out of place with the other appointments of the room. Amaryllis couldn't work out whether this family was very wealthy or very poor. Certainly not of the Nine Castles!

Further confusions followed. Hot water poured into basins at the pressure of a metal lever, voices and music blared from a small dark box. Chairs were luxuriously squashy, beds low and strange. Strangest of all was the privy. Amaryllis scarcely recognised it for what it was.

She ventured out to the grass and sniffed appreciatively. So that was the green herbal scent she had smelt earlier in the darkness. Newly cut grass. But how had anyone scythed it so short and smooth? Cautiously, Amaryllis sat down. The hound she had thought to be Red came bounding busily out from the shade of the house and leapt at her excitedly.

'Red,' she said softly. Since she was so strangely changed in this dream herself, why should this hound not be Red in another guise?

The hound settled on its haunches, head on one side, intelligent eyes fixed on Amaryllis' face. But the eyes were not Red's eyes and the mind behind was not programmed to give her companionship and safety. The dog whined, and the hair on its neck stirred into a ridge.

The hound knows, thought Amaryllis with a shiver. Even in a dream, the hound knows what the people do not.

'Red?' she said again in a low voice. 'It's all right, Red.'

The hound cringed. Amaryllis put out a hand and it broke away and fled.

'Hey!' said the voice of the boy who was not her brother. 'What'd you do to poor old Reg?'

# 5. AMY
## *Lady J*

The Great Chamber was enormous, as big as the memorial hall at home.

Bunching her skirts in her hands, Amy stepped cautiously under the arch. Something brushed against her, and she glanced down. The red dog was pacing at her side. She quickened her step, and tripped. Stupid! she said to herself. He can outwalk you. *He's* not wearing flowing robes!

The room appeared empty, but as she approached the table (big enough to seat a cricket team) she realised the chamber bent like a capital L. The short arm formed an alcove for a fireplace and chairs: high-backed straight seats with carved legs and backs.

In the alcove a woman stitched a tapestry, while a girl stood by with a basket of wool and thread. The woman was elegant and forbidding, her hair built into an elaborate style and covered with a gauze head-piece sewn with the same fiery gems that studded her

44

necklace. Her dress made Amy's look like a petticoat. Despite the clothes, hair style and bearing, she seemed familiar.

Amy watched her for a moment, then uttered a squawk of alarm as something brushed her hand. The dog. Again. As she edged away, the woman looked up, distaste flickering across her features.

'Amaryllis, how often have I bid you not to lift your skirts like a tower maid?'

Amy let her hem fall to the floor.

'Indeed,' said the woman. 'You are late. I must speak to Sophie: she was told to have you here betimes.'

'It wasn't Sophie's fault,' said Amy. 'I kept her talking.'

Lady Jasmin—for it had to be she—turned to the maid. 'Gillie, you may go. Tell my new sewing dame to attend me after we have eaten—should she feel sufficiently rested.'

When Gillie had gone, Lady Jasmin lightened her expression by a degree. 'You may be pleased to hear, Amaryllis, that your lord father and brother have returned.'

'Yes, Sophie said,' said Amy.

Lady Jasmin pounced. ' You have been gossiping?'

'It wasn't Sophie's fault,' said Amy. 'I asked her.'

Lady Jasmin sighed. 'Doubtless,' she said. 'Amaryllis, you must try for more conduct. It is unbecoming for a daughter of the Nine Castles to gossip with tower maids. Yet I shall not chide you more. You supervised the bundle making admirably yestereve. The maids evidently respect you despite your laxity of manner, and you have paid more heed to my wishes this last season.'

'Oh, good,' said Amy inadequately.

'Thank you, Lady Mother,' prompted Lady Jasmin. Amy blushed and felt she had let Sophie down. This was one response she should have remembered.

'We must discuss this lapse later,' said Lady Jasmin. 'Come, it is ill-bred to keep our menfolk waiting.'

Amy stared. This dreamworld of hers had attitude problems. If it was a dreamworld. If not, *she* had problems. Like that dog, which seemed to think it was attached to her by an invisible leash.

Childishly, she longed for crazy Reg. And for Jan and Mike. Even for horrible Craig! Biting her lip, she followed Lady Jasmin's regal progress around the angle of the wall. And the dog followed her.

The great polished table had been transformed with a cloth the size of a king-sized sheet and enough silver and earthenware to stock a china shop. Amy's eyes bulged at the splendour.

At the head of the table stood a man dressed in a peculiar pair of close-fitting trousers, a high-necked shirt with great full sleeves and actual lace down the front. Over it rippled a fine wool cape shot with crimson and wine. Not quite Superman: more Three Musketeers. He smiled, and Amy thought he looked a little like Mike—although Mike was not one for fancy dress. Or for little pointed beards.

'How fares my Ryllis?' asked Lord Michael kindly. A silver chain glinted around his wrist as he took her hand. 'Still hungering for a sight of Western Port?'

Amy nodded silently. It seemed safest.

Lord Michael kissed his wife's hand in greeting. Amy

stared, visualising Mike's habit of giving Jan a morning cuddle in the kitchen. But maybe Lady J wasn't the cuddling sort.

'I trust your new sewing dame is to your satisfaction?' said Lord Michael.

'As to that,' said Lady Jasmin, 'I shall inform you when she has proved her worth. You had no trouble with her hire?'

'None,' said Lord Michael. 'She was most willing to attend a lady of the Fifth Castle.'

Lady Jasmin nodded as if that went without saying. 'And where,' she enquired coolly, 'is Crag? Is he not aware of the time?'

Lord Michael looked grim. 'He will not be long,' he said, in a voice that implied that Crag had better not be. 'Be seated, my lady.'

He lifted back one of the carved chairs and Lady Jasmin subsided into it gracefully, flicking her skirt so that it arranged itself in a crimson curtain and concealed the legs of the chair.

Wowissimo, thought Amy, and sat down. She tried to get her skirt to do the same trick, but Lady Jasmin was looking at her with disapproval. *Now* what?

'Amaryllis, how often have I bid you to wait until you have been seated?'

'I'm sorry.' Amy trod on her skirt as she tried to get to her feet. Luckily, Lady Jasmin's attention was distracted by the flurried entrance of a boy, who sat down in a vacant seat with a muttered apology. Lady Jasmin eyed him coldly. 'Crag, it is correct to seat your sister first. Take care. She is all awry this morning.'

The boy bit his lip, but took Amy's arm and guided her into her seat. Beside her, the dog sank to its haunches.

'Thank you,' she said shyly.

Glancing up sideways, she received almost the worst shock since she had first woken to this strange situation.

The boy they called 'Crag' looked just like Craig: *was* Craig—bony face, speckled grey eyes, flopping light hair and all.

Her heat gave an enormous thump.

Could it be Craig—really her brother Craig—caught up in this mad game of All Change alongside her?

Throughout that strange breakfast, Amy kept glancing hopefully at the boy.

Was it Craig? The features were the same, the hair grew in the same ragged way across the boy's forehead. The expression was familiar: Amy had often seen that mulish look on Craig's face. Even the hand that this boy stretched out for the dish of steaming rolls (obviously just baked) looked like Craig's. The hand was long, narrow and callused, and the nails were bitten.

So Amy gazed and gazed at the boy's face, waiting for some tiny sign, some glance or nod to tell her that it really was her brother and she wasn't alone.

It never came, and it finally occurred to her that perhaps Craig—if it were he—didn't recognise her. After all, she was more changed than he, with her long gleaming braid of hair and sweeping skirts. Not to speak of an attendant guard dog.

Her chance came when a maid silently passed her a dish of cooked fish. It seemed an odd thing to have for breakfast, but the other items on the table were odd too—Amy averted her gaze from a plate of steaming kidneys.

'Greatissimo,' she said deliberately, and crossed her fingers, hard. The boy stared at her, but with no sign of germinating comprehension.

Lady Jasmin stared also, less concerned with what Amy had said than with the fact that she had spoken at all.

To avoid her coldly enquiring gaze, Amy sneaked another look at the boy who could not, after all, be Craig. For Craig would have registered comprehension in some way or another. He was impossible, he was unbearable, but he wasn't dim-witted. And Craig would never have helped her to a seat without giving her a sly pinch to be going on with. She had angered Lady J for nothing.

Crag, then.

This boy was Crag, and her own invention.

It all slotted in, in a crazy sort of way. She had invented a story, a tale, a whole different world called Ankoor— just for fun. And now it seemed she had woken into her own story. Well, more or less.

She felt a light pressure against her leg and glanced down. The dog was leaning against her. To intimidate her? To warn her? To comfort her? Daringly, she reached down to touch the domed head. Her fingertips tingled and she jerked away. He was a spellhound, after all. She had decided that—but she hadn't thought it through. Just what *was* a spellhound? What could it do?

'Amaryllis!'

'I'm sorry, Lady Mother,' she said hastily, and rubbed

49

her fingers hard against her skirt. After a moment she felt a soft heavy weight as the dog put its chin on her knee. Just like Reg when he was feeling soppy! So it seemed that the creature was on her side, like Sophie the maid. Lord Michael seemed to like her, too, unlike Lady J. And the boy—Crag—where did he fit in? She'd made him wicked in her first story—but she hadn't written that bit down. She'd hardly written anything, really—just a few names and places—enough to fix them in her mind.

Amy's face cleared. That must be the key! She'd been thinking about her story just as she went to sleep. So tonight, when she went to bed in the tower room, she'd think hard about her real life. Then she'd wake in her own bed in the morning and that would be that.

And she'd never play the going-to-sleep game again!

Heartened by the thought, she gave her attention to breakfast. It struck her that it was unwise to eat the food of another world—look at what happened to Thomas the Rhymer and Persephone! But it was too late now, and so she wouldn't think about it. Having decided that, she thought of little else until Lady's Jasmin's chill voice interrupted.

'And now, my son, you will entertain your sister and myself with the tale of your adventures at Western Port.'

It was obvious that Crag had no such wish, but his mother was looking expectant. He raised one shoulder in a very Craig-like shrug.

'Come, Crag. Something of note must have occurred,' said Lady Jasmin bracingly. 'Perhaps you visited the Fair Hall and inspected the registry there?'

Amy squirmed in silent sympathy, just as she did at

home when Jan or Mike tried to extract information from a clam-like and reluctant Craig.

Crag inserted a large piece of roll into his mouth and munched silently.

'Crag!' snapped Lord Michael. 'Answer your lady mother!'

Crag swallowed. 'We rode westward for many hours, Lady Mother,' he said deliberately. 'I wore my new garments as you bade me. My nether parts were rubbed almost raw in consequence. We passed far through the estate and spoke to many herdsmen and saw so many reinbeast my eye is blurred still with their movement. We so came to Western Port, avoided the many brawling drunken fellows making merry and fell in with Lord Damon of the Eighth Castle.'

Lady Jasmin nodded. 'I hope you attended him well,' she said. 'The Lord Damon is a cultivated person and a good template for such a lad as yourself.'

'The Lord Damon,' said Crag deliberately, 'is a drunken sot. I confess to prefer Lord Random of the Tenth Castle, who was there also, and who showed considerably more . . .'

'That will do, Crag,' said Lord Michael in a steely voice. 'We recognise Nine Castles only at this board.'

Crag bowed his head. 'Lord Father conducted business at the port, Lady Mother, and hired a sewing dame who is as plain of visage as you would wish. We spent the night at a western inn of repute. There we came upon Master Ash, a most cultured man, master of harp and lute.'

'A foolish jester,' said Lady Jasmin.

'A most cultured man,' repeated Crag without insolence. 'We fell to conversation, and the master made remark that he seeks an apprentice at the Great Fair . . .'

'Indeed,' said Lady Jasmin, 'and what has that to do with a son of the Nine Castles?'

'Lady Mother, I have no aptitude to follow in Lord Father's ways, no skill with the estates, no eye for good reinbeast stock,' said Crag. 'May I not follow my own . . .'

Lady Jasmin rose to her feet. 'My son—a tinkling musician? My son—a common minstrel?' she said scathingly. 'And what of the Fourth Castle in time to come? With no son of the blood to manage the estate and uphold the emblem?'

'My lord father could take an apprentice,' mumbled Crag.

'Never in the history of the Nine Castles!' thundered Lady Jasmin. 'You must have lost your wits entirely, Crag, lost them among the common company you keep. No, my lord!' she swept on as Lord Michael tried to intervene, 'I had thought better of you! To allow our only son to traffic in such company, such foolish notions—I lay this at your door, my lord, make no error! And shall it not be on your head and the head of your ancient name?'

She sailed out of the Great Chamber.

'Thus speaks the false pride of the Fifth Castle,' cried Crag angrily, but Lord Michael had had enough.

'I depended upon you, Crag, to say nothing to disquieten your lady mother,' he said reproachfully. 'You have shamed me.'

Crag thrust aside his plate. Lord Michael turned to

Amy, visibly shifting his mood. 'And how fares my Ryllis? You have kept your silence unusually. Are you well?'

Amy nodded, not daring to speak.

'What, no voice to beg a ride to Western Port? No news as to how our affairs go? No wish to hear what plans we did make for the Great Festival?'

Oh-oh, thought Amy. Here's the crunch. I'm going to get caught out if I'm not careful. She tried to look intelligent, and smiled.

Lord Michael looked surprised, so she must have miscued already.

Whether he meant to or not, it was Crag who rescued her. 'Sister Amaryllis is wiser than her brother, it seems,' he muttered. 'She knows that what she says will dismay her elders, so she says nothing at all.'

'That her elders were so wise,' said Lord Michael with a snap. 'I must be off. Several of the does of the East Craglands should now be with young, and I have the faintest of hopes that one may be coloured with a lost shade. Would you dice on our chances, Crag?'

Crag looked helpless. 'That would please you, Lord Father?'

'Aye,' said Lord Michael. His voice was very dry. 'And you, my son? Would that please *you*?'

Crag said nothing, and after a while Lord Michael turned ruefully towards Amy. 'And you, my Ryllis? Your lady mother speaks well of your conduct and you have no lessons while Master Greenhaven attends his father. What do *you* say? Will you ride with me today in hope to the craglands?'

Amy wanted to accept, for she would have liked to have seen the reinbeast—whatever they were. But she would be bound to give herself away. She shook her head. 'My lady mother said her sewing lady was coming to make me a blue coat,' she said apologetically. 'No, a mantle. That was it. Perhaps I can see the animals later?'

Lord Michael looked at her oddly, then nodded. 'Be off then, child, and appease your lady mother. Perhaps that is best.' He and Crag left the table.

Amy blew out her cheeks wearily and mopped her forehead with her sleeve. It was just past breakfast time and already she was exhausted.

# 6. AMARYLLIS
## *Witch*

maryllis was shocked. She had done nothing to the hound. She shrank against the bushes, but the boy was confronting her with angry eyes. 'What'd you do to old Reg, El Creepo?'

'I did nothing,' said Amaryllis.

'Nothing! Look at him!' exclaimed the boy. The hound was cowering some distance away. As she watched he shifted his paws and licked his lips, whining.

'Nothing at all,' said Amaryllis huskily. With the boy who looked like her brother and the hound who resembled Red accusing her, the dream was once again a nightmare.

'Well, watch it, El Creepo, that's all!' The boy lifted his fist, then turned away.

Amaryllis' mouth trembled. She had taken Red's devotion for granted: the spellhound was her friend as well as her guardian. Why did his other self fear and hate her so? *Was* she witched? Did he sense it? Yet this animal—this Reg—lacked the finely tuned senses of a spellhound. Red had the tactile aura of the Seventh Castle; this poor animal radiated nothing but confused horror.

'Amy! Aaaa-my! Come and do your room!' called the woman.

Amaryllis went cautiously into the cottage. Jan was using a cleaning device on the floor: where it passed, bits of lint vanished.

It was like a dragon, thought Amaryllis in awe. Like some greedy dragon leaving clear ground in its wake.

'There!' said Jan as the throaty roar died away. 'Now pick up all your things and put them away. *Away*, Amy, not bundled in the cupboard!'

Amaryllis looked around in bewilderment.

Tidying a chamber was a tower maid's task, not for a daughter of the Fourth Castle. But then, in the minstrel's tale she had made she had repudiated the Nine Castles . . .

Amaryllis picked up a ledger. She lingered over its fine binding and the wonderful engravings inside, then placed it reverently with its fellows in a shelf.

The bedsheets were gone, and as Amaryllis worked, a man carried in some others.

Following the crazy logic of the dream, the man looked somewhat like Lord Michael, but his garments were so uncouth she blushed to look at them and his face was shaven like a peasant's.

'Morning, chicken,' he said cheerfully. 'Having a bit of a tidy-up?' Amaryllis nodded, and bent to her tidying with new energy. Two more shiny ledgers were rescued from beneath the table and another from the top. On this Amaryllis' hand lingered wistfully, for it was bound in green and figured in gold and it reminded her of the ledger she had found in the coffer attic.

'Finished?' Jan put her head round the door. 'Put those books in the shelf and then run outside. Don't forget your hat.' She jammed a wide-brimmed cap on to Amaryllis' head.

Startled, Amaryllis thrust the ledgers among the others on the shelf and left the chamber. She wandered across the grass once more, alert for a sight of the red hound. He must have been equally alert for her, for she caught sight of a frantic tail vanishing among the greenery. She sighed and lifted her gaze. The sky seemed wider and bluer than that of her waking world and it was warm—so warm.

The trees grew tall and straight here, and the grass was fine and lush as moss. It was a gentle place, without craglands, rock or treacherous ocean. Amaryllis passed beyond the bushes to a thicket of fruiting canes. She hesitated, then drew back. The fruit might be witched or belong to some other castle. It might be poison, and if she died in this dream, who knew if she would wake again? Her hand rose to her birthchain for protection, but it was not there. Her other hand groped for the spellhound, and found emptiness.

Something moved beyond the barrier, and Amaryllis looked up to see a girl dismounting from a two-wheeled conveyance.

The stranger looked to be about her own years, so Amaryllis smiled. The girl sneered and Amaryllis gaped in surprise. She had done nothing to this person! But then, she had done nothing to the red hound. Nothing but exist in this state of wrongness which he sensed but could not alleviate.

'Seven days, Day, seven days,' said the girl darkly, and whirred away.

Seven! thought Amaryllis. Seven was the witch number, the number of the Seventh Castle. A feeling of dread settled in her chest. The sun seemed furnace hot and perspiration ran freely down her back. Was the Seventh Castle behind this dream? To be sure, great good came of the Seventh Castle, but the balance was great evil.

'*There* you are, Amy!' said Jan's voice from behind her. 'Wasn't that your friend Sharon?'

Amaryllis shook her head. No friend would address another like that.

'Really? It looked like her.' Jan looked at her thoughtfully. 'Best go in for a while,' she advised. 'You're a bit pale. Feeling OK?'

'Your pardon?' said Amaryllis.

'Are you all right? Not feeling sick or anything?'

Amaryllis shook her head and went into the cottage.

The sun was almost overhead when a roaring carriage slowed and halted at the gate. Amaryllis was enchanted and came out to see. Here was the conveyance of her tale!

A woman climbed out of the carriage with a grunt. She wore skirts, ending outlandishly below her knees. Even more outlandish was the way she strode up the path and flung her arms around Amaryllis, almost lifting her off her feet. 'Amy!' she boomed. 'You're a sight for sore eyes, luv! Got a kiss for old Gran?'

Amaryllis stepped away hastily. 'What's up?' said the

woman. 'Not turning into a teenager all of a sudden are you?'

Jan was closing the gate behind her and stopped to shake her head at Amaryllis. 'Don't mind Amy, Gran,' she said. 'She's not quite herself.'

She dropped her voice and Amaryllis caught a few disconnected words: 'Overslept . . . seems quite . . .'

'Is she *going* regularly?' demanded the older woman. 'Been eating cheese? Fair bungs you up, cheese does.'

'Come on, Gran,' said Jan, 'let's get out of the heat.'

'Out of the neighbours' earshot, you mean,' said the gran with a shrewd chuckle.

'Yes indeed, you wicked old woman,' said Jan.

The gran laughed delightedly. 'Amy doesn't mind if her old gran's a bit outspoken, do you, chick?' she said. 'Better than being mealy-mouthed, I always say.'

'Nothing like practising what you preach,' murmured Jan.

Amaryllis smiled cautiously, liking Gran's cheeky wink. Her lady mother would have thinned her lips and assumed deafness. Lord Michael might have been amused, but he would have hidden it politely, and Crag—what would Crag have done?

Amaryllis knew that her brother had a secret repertoire of rollicking broad ballads collected from some of his more dubious acquaintances and practised in private. Ballads to drink and dance to, fit for roaring log fires and roaring company. Yes, Crag might have appreciated the gran.

'And where's that lazy man of yours?' demanded Gran, entering the kitchen. 'Cooking lunch? I'd best watch out for cyanide in the salad!'

The man who looked like Lord Michael nodded at her solemnly. 'You got here, I see,' he said pleasantly. 'Must have smelt the food.'

Jan was stirring something in a jug, and now she tasted it and made a wry face. 'Gran, I think it's curdled. See what you can do.'

'Probably make it curdle worse,' said Mike out of the corner of his mouth. 'You know what they say about witches and milk.'

Amaryllis stiffened. A witch! And she in this dream with neither birthchain nor spellhound! Did Mike not know how dangerous it was to mock a witch? Even Gillie's grandam, a respectable purveyor of charms, had to be treated with caution.

What would happen if the woman sensed her for a stranger? If the witch knew, yet chose not to speak, then Amaryllis would be in the witch's power.

The gran took a wooden spoon and beat the contents of the jug, muttering an uncurdling charm as she worked. A kitchen crone then, like Gillie's grandam. And now Amaryllis came to look at her closely . . . ah! The grandam had the stigmata of the Seventh Castle: the odd-hued eyes! No kitchen crone she, but one born to the power.

'Amy? Run and call Craig for lunch,' said Jan.

Amaryllis, relieved to be out of the witch's aura, found the boy on the porch with the red hound. 'Whatcha want, Creepface?' asked the boy.

'She—Jan—said to call you for lunch,' said Amaryllis carefully. 'But take care: the gran is there—the witch.'

Her eyes sought the red hound's and it cowered and whined.

Craig stared at her. 'Eh?'

'The crone,' repeated Amaryllis faintly. 'The grandam. She has eyes of blue and green!'

Craig laughed. 'Weird. El Creepo, weird,' he said, and circled his ear with a finger.

A warding-off?

'The sauce, the sauce in the jug,' said Amaryllis in a low voice, ''tis curdled.'

'*You're* flamin' curdled,' said Craig, shoving her. 'Move. I'm starving. C'mon, Reg!' But the hound was slinking away.

Amaryllis could scarcely eat. The old woman kept staring at her with her mismatched gaze and asking questions. Why had Amy not been to visit her lately? When was Amy going to come? Was she too busy with her friends to have time to spare for poor old Gran?

Out of the corner of her eye, Amaryllis saw Jan shake her head.

'What's that?' said the gran abruptly. 'Am I sticking my foot in it somehow? Out with it, Jan, I'm not a bloody mind-reader.'

Jan seemed unintimidated. 'It's not you that Amy doesn't want to see, is it, love?' she said, raising her eyebrows at Amaryllis. 'It's Caz.'

'The Brandon girl? A real little madam, that one, but Amy and her are thick as thieves.'

'Were,' said Jan, very drily indeed. 'And no, I don't know what happened. Amy won't say.'

'Well!' said the witch, 'I'll get it out of her. C'mon, Amy.'

Amaryllis trailed miserably out to the porch. The gran sank with a grunt onto the sun-warmed boards and patted the spot beside her. 'Fell out with your friend, did you?' said the witch abruptly. 'Tell old Gran.'

Amaryllis edged away. 'How many years have you?' she asked respectfully.

The gran chuckled. 'Oh, about 392.'

Amaryllis stared.

'Not talking?' said the gran. 'Hardly the Amy we all know and love!'

Amaryllis froze. The witch knew. 'You are right,' she said in a low voice. 'I am Amaryllis Loveday, of the Fourth Castle. I am dreaming and you have discovered me. The hound knows, but the others do not.'

The witch raised her brows. 'What's this? Something you've got off the telly? Or—'

Amaryllis' hand went to her birthchain to ward off the witch's strange eyes. But the birthchain was not there. ''tis true!' she cried.

The old woman stared. 'Buggermecharlie!' Abruptly she heaved herself to her feet. 'Oy, Jan! Better have Amy lie down,' said the witch. 'She's got a touch of the sun. Rambling away like Jon-the-cop did after that Lamb woman heaved the rolling pin at him. Silly young fool, barging in on a domestic!'

So Amaryllis was bustled away by a concerned Jan, had her face sponged with cool water and was tucked into a freshly made-up bed. A curtain was drawn, and a vessel of cold sweet liquid put beside the bed. 'You go off to sleep, Amy,' Jan said kindly. 'You'll feel better when you wake up.'

'I'm sure I shall,' whispered Amaryllis. Just for a moment, the red hound's muzzle poked around the door. It twitched and withdrew.

'I am sorry, sorry to afear you so,' murmured Amaryllis. She closed her eyes, and bade the confusing dream a thankful goodbye.

# 7. AMY
## *Sewing Dame*

my lifted aside the tapestry hanging and started up the steep spiral stair, the hound at her heels. By now she was accustomed to his presence and almost welcomed it—though the slight fizz of his touch still made her pause.

After three spirals, they came to a landing. The floor was rough, as if the rock had been split along the natural fissures instead of smoothed into precise paving stones.

'Sophie!' she called softly. 'Sophie? Where are you?'

The tower maid appeared, finger to lips.

'Hush, Miss, and come to the coffer attic,' she said softly. 'Gillie will come in a little moment. She is gone to her grandam in the village.'

'Why does this staircase go through my room?' asked Amy curiously as they climbed. 'Is that a servant's room or something?'

'No, no, Miss, the spiral leads through all chambers:

it must, else how could we tower maids do our early work?' As she spoke, Sophie lifted the latch of a small wooden door and they entered a room lined with metal-banded chests. Amy moved to peer out through one of the slit windows.

'Wowissimo!' she said in awe.

The coffer attic was immensely high, and she could see a panoramic view of a bleak sea washing on a bleaker shore. Seabirds dived about the cliffs, and away to the left were rocky crags where animals grazed. And such animals! Too big to be sheep, a little like horses—not really like either—and blue! Or at least, bluish. Could they be llamas? Blue llamas?

That's where the wool comes from, decided Amy. And they dye it before they shear the sheep! Grossissimo!

She found Sophie hovering at her shoulder. 'Miss, no time for gazing,' she said. 'Tell me quick before Gillie comes. Have you indeed forgotten yourself, or is it some supposing game?'

'It isn't a game,' said Amy. 'I only wish it was. But I haven't forgotten myself, Sophie. Not the way you mean. I told you earlier, I'm not Amaryllis Loveday. Amaryllis Loveday is someone I made up. I think. The only thing is—if this is a dream or an hallucination, shouldn't I think I'm her? Oh, dear.'

Sophie looked puzzled—and no wonder, thought Amy wildly. She was sure she'd have looked puzzled if anyone at home—say like Caz or Sharon when they had still been friends—had tried out a story like this. It sounded like one of those madly detailed movie plots that were so confusing if you missed the first half hour.

(Could Caz have something to do with this? Of course not. Caz dealt in reality. 'You think about it,' said Caz in her memory. 'If you don't turn up on the 13th, you're out of the gang. Is that what you want?')

'Oh, Miss, you're witched for sure!' said Sophie. 'For I know well you're Miss Amaryllis Loveday and have been always: have I not known you these five seasons? Have we not been silent friends this long while? And never think 'tis not true friendship for all its silence. You're testing me perhaps?'

'No, no no!' cried Amy as warmly as she could. She liked Sophie, and it was cruel to make her unhappy, even in a dream adventure. 'I'd never do that. I mean, she wouldn't—if she really exists. I'm *not* her, that's all.' She shook her head and the heavy braid bounced, reminding her that, outwardly, she was. Her head spun. 'It's all right, really it is,' she said. 'I've thought about it and I'm sure I'll get home tonight.'

'But here is Gillie,' said Sophie with relief. The maid who had held Lady Jasmin's tapestry wool entered the attic.

'We must be quick,' said Gillie. 'Lady Jasmin has bid me send Miss Amaryllis to her betimes.'

Sophie waved this away. 'Have you the charm, Gillie? For certain there is something wrong, though the hound seems little enough alarmed.'

Amy took the chance to clarify something. 'What's he supposed to do?' she asked, indicating the dog. 'And what's his name?'

'Miss, Red is your guardian, to warn you of ill—as

powerful a charm as your birthchain,' said Sophie
seriously.

Amy almost smiled, despite her confusion. Lucky
necklaces and a magic dog! She loved it! And Red? Of
course. She had named him after Reg—almost. 'This?'
she said, fumbling behind her neck for the catch. Oddly
enough, there didn't seem to be one, and the chain would
not come over her head.

'Miss! Miss!' Never seek to take it off!' Sophie actually
sprang forward to grasp Amy's hands. 'You must never
remove the birthchain: 'tis your best protection!'

Gillie nodded seriously, and produced a small dark
object wrapped in gauze from her apron. 'Indeed, Miss,
you must be witched to try it.'

Sophie removed a needle and thread from her round
white collar. 'Turn back your skirt, Miss,' she said
briskly.

'Whatever for?' said Amy. She didn't like the look of
the needle, which was curved and businesslike.

'To fasten the charm,' said Sophie.

'But what is it?' demanded Amy, putting out her hand.
'Haven't I got enough already?'

Gillie handed over the gauze bag. 'The birthchain
wards off evil,' she said, 'as the spellhound warns of its
presence. This charm of my grandam drives evil away.
Do not fear, Miss; Grandam is a kitchen crone, and not
of the Seventh Castle! See? The hound knows its virtue!'
And indeed the animal did appear to be taking a great
but mannerly interest in proceedings. At the sight of the
dark thing, his plume of a tail waved gently.

Amy patted him and sniffed. The charm smelled of cloves and cinnamon and eucalyptus.

'It'll keep the moths away, anyhow,' she said with a shrug.

Gillie nodded seriously. 'And much else beside. A never-failing charm 'gainst dark witchery, my grandam did say.'

'I suppose she's a witch herself,' said Amy rather wildly, as she turned back her skirt. Gillie nodded again, with pride.

'There, 'tis done,' said Sophie, snapping off the thread. 'And before you sleep, I shall stitch it to your bedgown.'

The two maids smiled with such relief in their eyes that Amy realised that to them this ritual was as real and beneficial as any dose of medicine. And who knew? There were more things in Heaven and Earth . . . But this place was neither Heaven nor Earth, and she felt apprehensive again. And that was ridiculous. If this was a world of her imagination, where was the danger?

'You will help me, until I go home—won't you?' she asked anxiously. 'And tell me what to do now?'

'Go with Gillie to the Great Chamber,' said Sophie. 'Your lady mother and the sewing dame wait to begin your winter mantle.'

Amy did not like the sewing dame. She was civil enough, but she had a harsh voice, her nose was sharp and her eyes glittered like twin jet beads. Her lips seemed permanently puckered from holding rows of pins and she smelled strongly of stale sweat. Amy reminded herself that the woman had had a long journey, and probably little sleep in a strange place, and that perhaps it was a bit much to expect her to begin work so early on her first day on the job, but it made little difference. Either you liked someone or you didn't, and this time she didn't.

Nevertheless, she stood obediently while dry and capable hands draped her in swathes of the luminous blue cloth, then tugged and nipped it into shape.

'Isn't it a pretty colour!' she said at one point, hoping to soften the atmosphere.

'Most becoming, Miss, oh, an excellent choice!' said the sewing dame.

'I have bespoken my kinsman to send stargems for the girdle,' said Lady Jasmin.

The sewing dame primmed her mouth until her lips disappeared.

'You object?' suggested Lady Jasmin.

'If it please you, my lady, I feel such gems would be inappropriate,' said the dame.

'It does not please me,' said Lady Jasmin.

'A child has no need of such finery,' muttered the sewing dame. ''tis ostentatious.'

'No need?' Lady Jasmin's voice dripped frost. 'And who may wear the stargem if not a lineal daughter of the Fifth Castle?'

She and the sewing dame stared at one another for a moment, and the dame's eyes dropped first. 'Your pardon, my lady,' she murmured, and drove in a pearly-headed pin. 'I misspoke myself.'

Amy cringed, but fortunately the mantle was a loose garment with a wide collar and loose sleeves. Nevertheless, she began to suspect that the sewing dame would not be too unhappy if a stray pin should penetrate skin instead of cloth.

It was clear that the woman also disliked Red, for her jet-bead eyes flickered at him now and then with an odd expression in their depths. Not quite fear or distaste, but—something. Red apparently returned her sentiments for, as the sewing dame bent to insert another pin in the hem of the mantle, he suddenly whined and lifted a dignified lip. His hackles stirred, and the strange, almost electrical field about him intensified. Amy stared at him in bewilderment and the sewing dame's hands began to shake.

Gillie, standing by with the inevitable basket of tapestry wools, gasped audibly.

Lady Jasmin's straight form became straighter and she gestured at the sewing dame to stand back. 'Leave the mantle, and this place,' she said abruptly. 'Collect what is owed you from the steward and never return.'

The sewing dame's face twisted. 'My lady, my words on the trimming may have been ill-advised . . .'

'It is not your words, but your intentions which are unacceptable,' said Lady Jasmin. 'Go. But first . . .'

She nodded abruptly to Gillie, who helped Amy out of the mantle and draped it hastily over a chair.

' . . . first,' repeated Lady Jasmin, 'remove whatever unsavoury charm you have affixed to the garment hem.'

''tis nothing, nothing but a luckpiece,' protested the sewing dame. Red growled and she bent and removed the pin she had placed last.

'Then you'll not object to affixing it to your own gown,' suggested Lady Jasmin.

The sewing dame's eyes dropped. ''tis not for the likes of me.'

'Indeed.' Lady Jasmin turned to Gillie. 'Run, Gillie, and fetch me Hollies. He will escort this woman from the castle.'

There was a long uneasy pause as they waited for the maid's return. Amy tried to make sense of the strange events. Then a grizzled man in rich brown leggings and cape stalked in. Lady Jasmin nodded, and the sewing dame, still protesting, was firmly led away.

Lady Jasmin sighed. 'Amaryllis, I had wished to spare you such scenes until you reached more mature years, but now I must be plain. As you are doubtless aware, some few misguided folk choose to resent our position and our advantages—well-earned though these have been. With most, this resentment goes no further than simply envy, yet there are others who seek to reverse our fortunes. They do not act openly against your lord father, but strike at the fabric of his life through—certain avenues.'

'Like me,' said Amy flatly.

'Indeed. So keep your spellhound close and heed his warnings.' She glanced down at the dignified Red and her face softened slightly. 'He is an excellent beast and he knows he has done well.'

Amy shivered and looked at the blue mantle. 'Is that safe to wear?'

Lady Jasmin's brow wrinkled with perplexity, but the spellhound was nudging Amy's hand. Of course!

'Red would know if there was any danger,' she ventured. 'Wouldn't he?'

Lady Jasmin's brow smoothed and she gave Amy an odd glance of something like respect. 'Indeed, if the spellhound is satisfied, there is nothing more to fear. But come now, it is time to study your deportment.'

The rest of the morning passed slowly. If there was any drama over the sewing dame's expulsion, Amy heard none of it, for Lady Jasmin kept her occupied with tiresome exercises. After lunch she took Amy with her to the village, where she distributed bundles to various cottages. Amy found this embarrassing, but the recipients seemed not to mind.

Bath time was a novelty: the bath was round and the taps like nothing she had ever seen. Amy suspected the plumbing was better than they had at home. While she washed, Sophie collected the enormous nightgown from the round room and skilfully mended the torn-off ribbon.

'And see, Miss, I've sewn the charm to your bedgown, just as I promised,' she said. ''tis as well to be certain.'

After the peculiar scene with the sewing dame, Amy was more inclined to take this seriously, and she smiled up at Sophie with real gratitude as the girl began to brush her hair.

'And are you well indeed now, Miss?' asked the tower maid hopefully as she secured the long braid.

'Much better thank you, Sophie,' said Amy. She crossed her fingers. 'In the morning I shall be my old self.'

After Sophic had gone, Amy lay down in the high bed and allowed her hand to trail over the edge to rest on the spellhound's smooth head. 'And thank *you*, Red,' she said. 'I'll be going home soon, but you will stay with me until then, won't you?' Her voice trailed off, and in the dark she rubbed the creature's ears in the way Reg always enjoyed. And perhaps by now, she thought hopefully, it really *is* Reg and that fizzing in my fingers is only pins-and-needles really and when I wake up . . .

Her thoughts began to eddy, and she slept.

# 8. AMARYLLIS
## *Second Awakening*

**I**n some ways the second awakening was worse than the first for Amaryllis. True, she no longer feared a fatal fever, but her conviction that this strange world of her invention was a dream was badly swayed. In a dream one did not sleep—or if one did, it was only to wake to cold everyday reality.

Miserably, she lay with her hands clasped behind her cropped head. It was daylight, but there seemed no reason to get out of bed. There had been no Red to guard her rest . . . suddenly she felt a childish anger. Why had not Red warned her of this? Why had he not somehow contrived to be with her in her exile? The only things which should have kept him from her were confinement or death . . .

Brisk footsteps approached, and Amaryllis turned her head quickly, half convinced that Lady Jasmin would enter to scold her for tardiness and self-indulgence. But of course it was Jan. Amaryllis turned her face away.

'You're awake!' Jan sounded pleased. 'You've slept right through the night! How do you feel now, Amy?'

Amaryllis shook her head silently.

'Oh.' Jan's voice was disappointed. 'Hungry?'

Amaryllis nodded. She was.

'Well, there can't be too much wrong then. I'll bring you in some fruit. Why don't you read?' Jan hesitated, then drew out a book. 'Here, try Paul Jennings. He's great to take your mind off things. Would you like me to bring old Reg in to keep you company? Craig's given him a flea-bath so it should be safe enough—if I put your slippers out of reach!'

Amaryllis shook her head in panic. She felt she could not face the hatred of the hound today. He was so like and yet so painfully unlike Red.

The fruit arrived in a pretty china bowl with a spoon, carried at arm's length by Craig. 'Here,' he said ungraciously.

It looked delicious, but Amaryllis hesitated. 'Well, take it!' said Craig impatiently. 'I'm not flamin' well going to feed you!'

'The—the old grandam did not prepare this?' asked Amaryllis in a low voice.

'Nah, she went home after you flaked it,' said Craig casually. 'I opened the tin with my own fair hands.'

'I thank you.' Amaryllis smiled shyly and began to eat. Craig rocked back and forth on his toes. 'Geez, you must be crook.'

It was a strange morning. Amaryllis stayed in bed, dozing and reading, doing her best to shut out the unwelcome world and fears of whatever witchment had brought her to this place and what might still be to come. Lord Michael had rivals, she knew: why else would he have provided her with the protection of a spellhound? The birthchained stargem should have been enough. Lady Jasmin vowed by that, yet it hadn't saved her daughter. Why had Red not howled a warning?

It seemed that someone—or something—had made use of the weavings of her own mind to entrap her. Not the grandam—she was of this world, for all that she bore the mystic eyes. It must be someone else.

Yet, thought Amaryllis, the old woman was grandam to the girl Amy, so who knew what revenge she might take on the one who had displaced her?

Craig came at midday with another bowl of food: a creamy syllabub of a type she had never tasted. Sardonically, he watched her eat.

Amaryllis wished him away. His presence was much more unnerving than that of Jan or Mike. They, she felt, thought she really *was* their daughter Amy. She wasn't so sure about Craig.

Craig was alert, like her brother Crag. Not one to be distracted from a puzzle.

'What's up with you anyway?' he challenged. 'Gutsache? Can't be. You're still eating.' His light grey eyes watched her intently.

Amaryllis slid under the bedsheets and closed her eyes with finality. He frightened her. His gaze was too intelligent. Too much like that of the grandam, although his eyes were both a speckled grey.

After a moment, she heard the door close, and cautiously opened her eyes.

'Gotcha, El Creepo!' said Craig in a triumphant undertone. 'Now—give.'

'What shall I give you?' asked Amaryllis warily. Was this boy a party to what had happened to her?

'Give. You know, *give*. Lowdown. Info. Tell big brother what you've done.'

'I do not understand.'

'Don't give me that!' said Craig roughly. 'Listen, El Creepo, this poor-little-Amy stunt might fool the wrinklies, but not me. What goes on?'

Amaryllis was silent. Did he know? Did he not?

'Look,' said Craig. 'Last time you played possum you'd been mucking about in my room and busted my amplifier. What is it this time? One of my speakers?'

'Nothing,' said Amaryllis stonily. 'Truly, Crag, it is naught.'

Immediately, she knew she had said something wrong. Craig's eyes narrowed, and he pounced and grabbed her by the shoulders. 'Listen, Creepface,' he hissed. 'There's something up all right and I'm going to find out what it is if I have to break . . .'

'Everything OK in here?' asked Jan brightly.

'Yeah, fine,' drawled Craig. 'Just fixing Amy's pillow for her, wasn't I, El Creepo? It was slipping down. Any further and *gkkkkk*.' He made an expressive rattle in his throat. 'Bye bye, little Amy.'

Jan put a cool hand on Amaryllis' forehead. 'Well that feels OK, Amy. How are you? Not going hot and cold? You can get up then, so long as you keep out of the sun. We don't want you ending up in hospital. By the way, Craig, Todd's waiting for you.'

"Yeah?' said Craig, not moving.

'*Craig.*'

'Coming,' said Craig. He leaned his hip against the bedside table, and Amaryllis' book thudded to the floor. 'Oh, hang on, sorry,' gabbled Craig. He bent slowly and as he retrieved the book, he glared at Amaryllis. 'You needn't think you're getting away with it, El Creepo, whatever it is!'

It seemed he *didn't* know.

After Craig had left, Amaryllis thought furiously.

Crag. She'd called him Crag.

Just a slip of the voice, but she couldn't afford another like it.

This Craig was the old witch's grandson, and who knew what powers he might have inherited? Gillie had none, but everyone knew that witchery, like colour density in reinbeast, was a chancy business.

And if this Craig indeed unmasked her, what then? Would he call for the old witch to send her helplessly to limbo?

Craig made several other attempts to catch her alone, but Amaryllis evaded him with the neatness of desperation, a feat equalled only by the red hound's avoidance of her. She hated to see such horror in the poor creature's gaze, and spoke to him sometimes from a distance. And gradually her efforts seemed to have their effect.

At first, she expected every morning to wake in the castle, but after three days of disappointment, she decided that waiting would achieve nothing. Of what virtue had waiting ever been? Had it earned her the journey to Western Port in Crag's stead? Had it given Crag permission to seek out a master of music?

The longer she waited this time, the more likely it was that Craig would confirm his suspicions and denounce her.

Outside the wilder minstrels' tales, most witches had limited power. Amaryllis knew those of the Seventh Castle could not turn her to a creeping cur, as the simpletons believed. And those who wore proper protection were almost wholly safe. Dark Ones entrapped only the unwary. Some snared their victims in webs of words, others made them will their own destruction, or drove them mazed with false visions. Bright Ones did none of this, yet it was well to have a care.

It must have taken great power to exile her to this world, and Amaryllis knew her birthchain should have held her to reality. And why had it been done? Was Lord Michael the real target?

If so, why had she been taken and not Crag? Crag was the logical one, the heir, the one who must carry the Fourth Castle into the next generation.

Amaryllis had no answer, but it was obviously her duty—whatever the danger—to break this thrall.

She couldn't do it alone.

For some time more Amaryllis sought for a solution. A countercharm from an equally powerful witch was the obvious route, but the only witch she knew of in this world was the grandam of Craig and the real Amy . . .

At night in the low small bed, Amaryllis tossed uneasily at the thought of the grandam. She knew it was the only answer, but kept putting it off, hoping that somehow she would be rescued. Her only consolation was that now the red hound no longer fled from her presence. Instead, he would hover at some little distance and gaze at her with dumbly pleading eyes, as if he sought for something or someone and saw in her a small chance of finding it. In some ways it was worse than before, for she felt herself as powerless to help him as she was to help herself.

Then Jan went into the city.

# 9. AMY
## Golden Fleece

my stretched, and opened her eyes.

Stone.

It hadn't worked. Her heart gave a huge, uncomfortable thud, and seemed to sink, just as it did when she woke at home and remembered Caz and the 13th.

But at least she needn't worry about Caz today. Where she was, Caz could never reach her. The thought was vaguely comforting, and so was the dark coppery muzzle that presently appeared over the edge of the bed.

'Yes, I'm still here,' she said to the spellhound. 'And I can see you haven't turned into Reg: he'd have been eating the pillow by now.' She sighed, hoping that Reg was not missing her too much. He was a sociable dog, and not too bright, but he always liked to keep his family in order and took it as a personal affront if one of them went missing.

While Amy was still trying to order her thoughts,

Sophie's smiling face appeared around the tapestry curtain. 'Morning, Miss!' she said cheerfully. 'We're betimes, today!'

'Good morning, Sophie,' said Amy.

'You slept well, Miss? No nighthags afeared you?'

Amy nodded. Nighthags were nothing, unless you woke to find them true.

Sophie said approvingly: 'There's naught like a true kitchen charm to fright off witchment.' She was in high spirits today, for she and Gillie had permission to ride to Western Port when Lord Michael went to the Great Fair.

''tis not the Fair I wish to see, Miss, though they call it a marvel, but that Jarman's ship will be in port. A short while only, else he'd have come to us here.'

'Jarman?' asked Amy.

'Why, Miss! My sweetheart and Gillie's brother besides, so 'tis doubly kind of your lord father.'

Amy eyed her with respect. Some of the girls at school had boyfriends, but these were a matter for giggles and blushes. Not to be taken seriously, like Sophie's.

'What am I to do today?' she asked apprehensively as the braiding was done. She had got away with it yesterday, but might not be so lucky today.

'Accounting maybe, with your lady mother,' said Sophie. 'You are fortunate indeed: most young ladies are able for naught but their stitchery. You will be fitted to run a great household, for all you'd wish it the estate.'

She chuckled ruefully and went away, leaving Amy to wonder what on earth she meant. Run an estate? Her?

She was going to be a writer! But then—she wasn't Amaryllis.

The spellhound was watching her intently, and Amy rubbed its ears. '*You* know the difference, don't you?' she said. 'But you still saved my bacon yesterday.' And she shivered, remembering the sewing dame's malevolence. Perhaps she'd been wrong about its being safer here . . . Perhaps there were things more dangerous than Caz . . .

Her stroking hand stilled and, for the first time, she thought seriously about the real Amaryllis Loveday. For there must be a real Amaryllis Loveday for Amy to have taken her place. And not only her place, but her body as well, right down to the lemon-butter plaits.

She wondered if the real Amaryllis would mind lending it, but came to the rather startling conclusion that she was probably lending her own body—to Amaryllis. They were even.

Amy wondered how a noble daughter of the Nine Castles would handle suburban Australia—*and* Craig— *and* Caz—and her mind boggled. But she hoped Amaryllis was there, and was handling it, because if not, Jan and Mike would be in a panic over their missing daughter. She bit her lip at the thought of their distress.

'Don't you ever get kidnapped,' Jan sometimes said. 'I'd never survive the suspense.'

But perhaps she wasn't missing. Perhaps when she did get home she'd find no time elapsed. That was what usually happened in time-travel stories, so she'd better hope it would happen for her.

But what about Caz? And what about the 13th? Better to hope the other Amaryllis—the real one—was hanging in there, trying to out-Amy Amy. And that she'd survive the 13th better than Amy would.

If I knew how I got here in the first place, thought Amy, maybe I could contact her. She thought of that last day at home. She had been bored and miserable on the porch.

She had helped Jan to sort the boxes.

She had lain in bed listening to the row and worrying about Caz.

She had played her old going-to-sleep game.

So far, so normal. She had done all those things many times before.

But she hadn't invented Amaryllis Loveday and the castle before. Had she invented them? Or had she somehow tuned into Amaryllis' world? Amy closed her eyes and concentrated fiercely on the image of a girl with long lemon-butter plaits, a flowing blue dress and a pale pointed face with grey eyes—but, no, she wouldn't look like that now! 'Amy to Amaryllis—Amy to Amaryllis, come in Amaryllis!' she muttered. It sounded stupid. She could just imagine what Caz would say.

'Amaryllis? Amaryllis?' she whispered. 'Can you hear me?'

Had what she'd written come true? Or had she written what already *was* true, in another time and place?

The spellhound stiffened beneath her hands, and suddenly she remembered the missing piece in the equation.

The green book! The book Jan had given her to use for 'something special'. She had written her Amaryllis story in that. Amy let out a long breath.

'Something special,' Great-Gran had insisted.

'Something special,' Jan had echoed.

'Something special!' said Amy to the spellhound. 'Was it ever! But it's there, not here. Or is it?'

Down on her knees by the coffer chest, Amy scrabbled through the contents. It took a couple of minutes to find what she half expected: a green leather book. Older, softer and more elegant than her own, but substantially the same. And there it was: the story of Amy Day as penned (surely) by Amaryllis Loveday . . .

The spellhound's hackles stirred a little. Danger? Or merely reaction to the strangeness within the book? Amy's hands shook, but she rested them on her lap. And as she began to read, it became plain what must have happened.

She had been half right. She *had* done this thing, but she hadn't done it alone. The real Amaryllis had also been writing, had also changed elements of her own life to create fiction. But *who* was in *whose* story?

Amy frowned, and her stomach churned. 'Well, *I'm* real,' she said firmly above the rattling noises. Gran would have advised a dose of salts to cure that. In Gran's opinion, a dose of salts cured most things.

'But it won't cure transplanting,' she said to the spellhound. 'And so I'll tell her when I see her next.'

Her face darkened a little as she remembered her last visit to Gran's—how she had seen Caz and Sharon at the pool and what Sharon had said.

'By the 13th, Day, or you're nothing.'

She would have to wait for Gran to visit *her*.

Nevertheless, she was satisfied that she knew her

route home. She had only to add to Amaryllis' story in the green leather book before she slept and that would whisk her back to her own life—and Caz. She felt a little sick at the thought. If only she could stay here until after the 13th . . . But she couldn't. It would be wrong to leave Amaryllis to face Caz while she lurked in safety. But is it so safe? she argued to herself. A place with bad charms and people like that sewing dame—maybe Amaryllis is as frightened of them as I am of Caz . . . maybe I'd be doing her a favour if I waited a while . . .

The door creaked open and she glanced up to see Sophie's face framed in the arch. 'Oh, Miss!' she said. 'What have you been doing?'

Amy looked sheepishly at the mess she had made of the coffer's contents and was ashamed. The things weren't hers to throw around. And Amaryllis' life wasn't hers to order. She had no right.

'I'll pick it up,' she said.

'Best let me, Miss. I've had practice!'

'I'm sorry,' said Amy. 'I didn't mean to make work for you. I was looking for this.'

She wagged the green book at Sophie, but the tower maid did not share her triumph.

'The ledger you took from your great grandam's chest in the coffer attic!' said Sophie. 'And what your lady mother would have said, to see you in the dust with that green ledger and the Bright Ones' wares about you, I dare not say!'

Amy took a deep breath. If she did it now there would be no chance to change her mind. 'Sophie,' she said firmly, 'This is the first time I've ever seen this book, but I have one like it, in my own world. I'm not Amaryllis—I'm Amy.'

Sophie's face puckered with distress. 'Miss, you have never taken off your charm so soon . . .? And it working to such good effect! Yestereve you said you were well . . . '

'Yes, but then I thought it was a sort of dream and I'd wake up. Now I know it's all because of this.' She held up the book.

Sophie nodded. 'If so,' she said soberly, 'best give the witched ledger to me. Gillie's grandam will know how best to draw its teeth.'

'You don't understand. Look!' Amy opened the book and thrust it in front of Sophie. The girl recoiled.

'No, read it!' Amy stabbed her finger at the lines so gracefully penned by Amaryllis.

'Miss,' said Sophie with reproachful dignity, 'you know I cannot.'

'Oh, Sophie!' Remorsefully, Amy snatched away the book. 'I never thought! Listen . . . ' She read the page aloud. 'That's what *she* wrote,' she said, 'and it's about me. And back home I wrote something about her! So if I add to her story now it will take me home.'

She would have done so right then, but a summons came from Lady Jasmin. So Amy, now wishing she'd held her tongue, resigned herself to one more day in the role of Amaryllis and left the tower chamber with Red.

Behind her, Sophie began, with shaking hands, to collect the scattered garments and return them to the coffer.

87

To Amy's surprise, Lady Jasmin seemed almost approving today. 'Amaryllis, I have a task for you, but first, I believe your lord father has some news of interest to you both. You may go to him until I send for you.'

Bemused, Amy went. She had no idea of Lord Michael's whereabouts, but luckily she met up with Crag, who had. Even luckier for her, he was too wrapped up in his grievances to wonder why his sister should be asking him how to find their father.

'In the stables, cosseting a reinbeast,' he said sourly, jerking a thumb in the appropriate direction. 'I would wish he showed as much concern over his own son.'

The boy's voice shook, and Amy frowned. Crag Loveday might *look* like Craig, but her brother would never have dropped his bundle like this. Craig would have fought to the end.

'I bet he does, really,' she said.

'Ah, go away, it is all of a piece,' said Crag. 'He'll doubtless be pleased to see *you*.'

'What about you?'

Crag turned away. 'If he'll not hear me, I'll not please him,' he muttered.

Amy sighed. But perhaps he had a point. Why shouldn't he learn music if he wanted?

Shivering in the brisk air, she crossed the courtyard, with Red pacing beside her. Was it summer here? If so, it was a curiously cold one, and from the look of the surrounding countryside it never got much hotter.

A sweep of sparse pasture ran like a tongue from the distant rocky crags to a walled and partially roofed yard:

presumably the stables where she would find Lord Michael.

Amy stepped through the arched opening, 'Lord Father?' she called. It sounded ridiculous. How Mike would have laughed.

'Ryllis?' Lord Michael's voice guided her to a stall. 'Should you not be about your duties?'

'Lady Mother sent me,' said Amy firmly. 'She said you had something to tell me.'

'Not tell—show!' said Lord Michael. 'But see what compliance has brought you? Protesting your lot as a daughter brings only disharmony. Your diligence yesterday has allowed this privilege. But look what we have here! A miracle!'

Amy, still puzzling over this speech (what *was* it the real Amaryllis kept nagging her parents about?), stepped forward. Gathering her unruly skirts, she stretched to see over the partition. At the sight of Lord Michael's 'miracle' she gave a gasp of pure delight.

'It is as we have hoped, you and I, Ryllis,' said Lord Michael. 'What my lord father and his strove for yet never achieved. A reinbeast of a lost shade. But no doubt you wish a closer view?' Going down on one knee, he offered the other as a mounting block. With only the slightest of hesitations, Amy scrambled over the partition to crouch enchanted by the baby reinbeast in the stall.

It had long spindly legs like a foal, but two nubby horns decorated its forehead between the fringed ears. The fleece was tightly curled and shone in the lantern light like wheat and copper.

Lurching forward, it nuzzled her fingers, bleating urgently. Amy was lost, and scarcely noticed as the spellhound and Lord Michael joined her in the stall.

'It's gold!' she breathed. 'A golden fleece!'

Lord Michael's voice echoed her delight. 'Indeed it is, and the first, I pray, of many! What do you say, daughter? Is this not an omen for the future? At last I may register our emblem in the flesh!'

# 10. AMARYLLIS
## *Blue Pool*

raig, are you doing anything special today?' asked Jan.

'You're joking,' said Craig flatly. 'What's to do round here?'

'Will you stay with Amy then? I don't like leaving her in case she takes another funny spell.'

'I'm going swimming at Jason's,' said Craig perversely. Then his eyes gleamed. 'But I s'pose El Creepo can come too. Want a swim, El Creepo?'

Amaryllis shook her head. 'No thank you, I shall stay alone.'

'That won't do,' said Jan. 'I'll be gone all day.'

'I shall come with you—'

'I'm going to the garage and then to the bank and Medicare and then I'm going to a gallery. You'd be bored stiff, Amy. You know you hate the city.'

'I shall come.' Amaryllis used the decided tone that sometimes won over Lord Michael.

'You? Pass up a swim?' Jan sounded astonished. 'Amy, what *is* wrong with you? Any other time you'd be pestering Craig to take you! Now he's offered, you go and be thankful.'

Amaryllis shook her head. She didn't trust Craig's offers.

'Yeah, I'll look after her,' said Craig readily.

Amaryllis saw that she was trapped.

'You'll like it at Jason's,' drawled Craig. 'Not too many bods in the water. I'll get in a bit of polo practice and you can do some dives.'

Jan nodded. 'You'll like that Amy!' she said, as if it had been she who had been offered the treat. 'Just don't overdo it . . . Yes, Craig, I know I'm fussing like an old chook, but you must admit she wasn't at all well the other day!' She glanced at the timepiece she wore on her wrist. 'I'll be off then. Home by six at the latest.' Jingling her car keys, she went out.

'Going somewhere were you, El Creepo?' asked Craig unpleasantly as Amaryllis turned to leave the kitchen.

'I am going to my room.'

'You are *going* to give me some straight answers. What have you done? Oh, blast it!' he added as the gate clinked open. 'Here's Jase already. But you'll keep, El Creepo.' He raised his voice. 'Yeah, hang about, Jase. Just gotta get me things off the line. By the way—she's coming too.' He jerked his head at Amaryllis.

'What? Your sister? Can she swim?'

'Our Amy's the original water rat, aren't you Ame? Wins championships and things. Under twelve last summer, under fourteen this summer, next year—the flamin' Olympics! C'mon.'

Reluctantly, Amaryllis found herself loaded with a bright tasselled towel and a wisp of shiny striped material and was swept off with the two boys. The red dog trotted after them, his hopeful eyes fixed on Amaryllis, but the other boy shook his head and said something.

'Yeah—OK,' said Craig. Turning back, he grasped Reg by the scruff of the neck and bundled him firmly— though not unkindly—back into the garden. 'And stay put,' he ordered through the gate. Reg thrust a pleading muzzle through the slats and then raised it to give an eerie howl.

Jason laughed. 'Hey—what's with him? Hound of the Baskervilles?'

'I reckon,' said Craig. Then he gave Amaryllis a brisk shove between the shoulderblades. 'Well come on, El Creepo. Get weaving.'

'The hound,' said Amaryllis huskily. 'Danger . . . '

'Don't be a meathead!' snapped Craig. 'Old Reg wants to come swimming, that's all. Only Jase reckons his wrinklies don't go a bundle on dog hair. They reckon it clogs the filter. Now will you come *on*?'

Amaryllis followed numbly, pursued by the red hound's howls of despair. The fair-haired girl who had sneered at her before pedalled past on her conveyance, staring. 'Four days to D Day, Day,' she said flatly. 'Be there.'

'What's that?' Craig had sharp ears, but Amaryllis ignored him—and the girl—and walked on.

The water was a most unlikely blue. Craig and Jason tumbled in, and began to play a furious ball game, sending up fountains with every throw and roaring about goals and misses.

Amaryllis watched them in disbelief. It was not cold here, but surely none but fools ever entered deep water.

A loud bell shrilled, cutting through the splashes and yells. Jason cocked his head. 'Phone,' he panted. 'Dad rigged up an outside bell. Gotta run. Here.' Thrusting the ball at Craig, he heaved himself out of the water and rushed off into the house.

'Coming in, Creepface?' Craig surged out of the water. 'Let's see that swallow dive you're always banging on about.'

Amaryllis shook her head decidedly. 'I do not wish to.'

'Eow, Ayee dew note weesh to!' mocked Craig. 'Well, guess what, El Creepo? You're going to.'

Amaryllis flinched as cold drops splattered her arms and face. Craig whipped away the towel, grabbed her arms, and propelled her towards the pool.

'No! No!' shrieked Amaryllis, but Craig scooped her up and threw her into the water.

# 11. Amy

## *Bright One*

Amy didn't write in Amaryllis' book that night. She certainly intended to do so, but somehow, over the span of the day, she changed her mind. After all, she knew how to get home now, and she could think of any number of reasons not to do so just yet.

At home, the rest of the holidays promised to be flat and tedious at best and, at worst, horrifying. She couldn't go to Gran's because of Caz. She couldn't visit Katie or Sharon or Barb, and they wouldn't visit her. Marina might, but Marina was a drip—and to join the gang she had had to drop her other friends. Caz had explained it all quite clearly. 'The thing is, Amy, you don't need friends any more, or even family. You've got us.'

That was the thing about Caz. She made things change. She made the rules and she meant what she said. She meant *more* than she said.

Amy had discovered that on the last day of school

when she had dared to tell Caz she didn't like Caz's latest idea for holiday thrills.

Last holidays the idea had been some harmless fun with the motorists along the highway.

'This is what we do,' Caz had told her acolytes. 'Dump your bike on the road, and when you hear a car, flop down and look as if you're dying.'

'That's fun?' Marina Ling had commented. No-one had spoken to Marina for a week.

They had staged three 'accidents' during the spring holidays, and Amy supposed it had been fun (of a nail-biting, gut-twisting sort) to hear the cars screeching to a halt.

'Teach them to drive a bit more carefully!' said Caz.

Then Marina had been a bit slow dragging her bike out of the way.

The bike had been crunched, the motorist had raged and demanded names and addresses, Marina had wept and Caz and the others had melted away.

Caz's code was simple.

Everyone for Caz first and herself next, and a solemn oath extracted from every gang member never to split.

Amy had run with the others, but she had felt sick about it, and but for her oath she would have broken with Caz and the gang right then. Not that she was afraid of divine retribution, but suddenly she *was* afraid of Caz. Particularly when she saw how Marina had been punished for her failure.

But Marina hadn't split, and things had gone smoothly until Caz had her next idea.

Again it was simple. One at a time, each ganger was to nick something from the mall.

'Those shops deserve it!' Caz had said quietly, and Sharon had backed her up.

'You know how they treat us! Serve wrinklies when we're in the shop first, give us crap when we touch anything! They're all crooks anyway. Geez, they put these huge profits on everything! Now *we're* going to score for a change.'

Caz had nodded gently. 'That'll teach them.'

Amy had gathered the courage from somewhere to oppose this scheme, and Sharon had turned on her like a taipan.

Either Amy did her bit, or else Caz—and Sharon—would fix her properly. And Amy knew they would. The others wouldn't help her. They hadn't helped Marina.

*She* hadn't helped Marina. When you looked at it that way, she deserved what was coming to her on the 13th.

That was what went through Amy's head as she replaced the green ledger in the coffer at the end of her second day at the castle. 'Don't worry, I won't let them hurt your Amaryllis,' she said aloud to Red as she climbed into bed. 'I'll go home tomorrow, I promise. I just want one more day. One more, and then I really will write myself home.'

Red gazed at her with quiet eyes, but Amy felt a blush surge up as if he had accused her. 'Tomorrow night. I promise,' she said, and blew out the lamp.

The next day, Lord Michael took Amy to a place he called West Craglands, high above the ocean. To her delight, she rode there in a sort of seat clamped to the back of a gelt reinbeast: an enormous and gentle beast covered with rough bluish wool. The spellhound and Lord Michael walked alongside, so Amy had nothing to do but sit there. Which was just as well, as her riding experience was nil.

When they reached their destination, the slighter blue reinbeast bounded down and came flocking around them, lipping and bleating for the salty snacks Lord Michael carried in his pouch. Their fleece, which at first appeared to be a uniform smoky blue, gleamed like shot silk with threads of rust, crimson and hints of gold, and Amy began to see dimly how difficult it must have been for Lord Michael to breed the little gold beast from such stock.

'Can we see more?' she asked eagerly as Lord Michael helped her to remount.

He shook his head. 'Let us not try the goodwill of your lady mother too far.'

She must have looked crestfallen, for he smiled and promised that another day, even perhaps on the morrow, they would visit the crimsons, her favourites, to choose a beast for the Nine Castles Pavilion at the Great Fair. Amy had to pretend to be satisfied, but she knew that, for her, tomorrow meant never.

Upon her return to the Great Chamber, Amy came to an abrupt halt in the angle of the L. Lady Jasmin had company, a pedlar woman in brilliant fluttering robes, her arms decked with bracelets and charms. A great shallow basket of wares rested at her feet, but she held herself like a fine lady and beckoned for Amy to come closer.

Glancing at Lady Jasmin for permission, Amy was astonished to see that lady fingering the birthchain at her throat. Hearing a whine, she glanced down at Red, and to her further astonishment she saw the spellhound's tail begin to wave and sensed his tension.

Hastily, she dropped a curtsey, practised during lessons with Lady Jasmin.

'This is Jadetha of the Bright Ones of the Seventh Castle, Amaryllis,' said Lady Jasmin as she approached. 'Bright One, our daughter Amaryllis and her spellhound, known here as Red.'

The other woman inclined her head, and held out a hand to Red. 'May I?'

Amy nodded, and removed her hand from the spellhound's ruff. The Bright One made a curious fluting whistle and Amy's mouth opened in a soft oh of astonishment as her dignified companion whined with delight and sprang forward to fawn like a pup at the Bright One's feet. The woman bent to fondle him and for a moment Amy felt the harsh pang of a jealousy to which she knew she had no right. Red owed *her* no loyalty. She wondered if he would have behaved so had she really been Amaryllis.

The Bright One glanced at her chagrined face. 'Your pardon, child of the castle,' she said in her lilting voice, 'but the hound and I are of old acquaintance. His grandam and mine roamed together in their youth.' She touched the spellhound's head. 'Ah, yes, my fine friend, you are a wonder, but return to your maiden now.'

Red came back to Amy with no trace of reluctance, but his eyes remained fixed on Jadetha.

'The Bright One visits the Great Fair at Western Port,' said Lady Jasmin abruptly.

Jadetha nodded and smiled a little slyly. 'And how should I not pause to meet with the kin of my kin?' Above the bright robes her skin was very pale and her eyes were odd-coloured: one blue and one green.

Wowissimo! Just like Gran's! thought Amy. But the Bright One was looking at her with equal attention.

'So you are another Amaryllis, like your grandam. And is Amaryllis the true daughter of this castle?'

Amy nodded, not trusting herself to speak, and the Bright One gestured for her to sit.

'Child of the castle, child of the crag, child of all the past,' she murmured, and her odd eyes seemed to see right down to Amy's soul. She conversed with Lady Jasmin for a time before suddenly bending to take up her heavy basket. From it, she took a strange coin which she handed to Amy.

'A luckpiece, child of the castle, child of the crag. Remember the Bright One, and surely the Bright One will remember you. And keep the spellhound close. He is more to you than you understand.'

Amy curtsied once more, and somehow fumbled the coin as she put it in the pouch of her dress. It bounced on the stone floor, ringing like silver. Amy winced, and it seemed that Lady Jasmin turned pale, but Jadetha merely smiled and went on her way.

The spellhound's eyes followed the bright figure with

a wistfulness that tugged at Amy's heart, but it seemed that Lady Jasmin was relieved to see her go. Her colour came back in a tide.

Lord Michael's reaction to the visitation was equally puzzling. He came in a few moments later and looked around with caution. 'The Bright One is on her way, then,' he said.

'Indeed,' said Lady Jasmin, her fingers straying again to the stargem at her throat.

'I am relieved,' said Lord Michael. 'I fear that the Bright One will one day request a pair of prime reinbeast and that I shall be tranced into giving them to her.'

From the light way he said it this might have been a joke, but Amy felt that it wasn't, quite, for his fingers were playing nervously with the birthchain at his wrist.

'The Bright One has given Amaryllis a token of the Seventh Castle,' said Lady Jasmin.

Lord Michael glanced at Amy. 'Indeed? But has she not one already in the hound?'

Lady Jasmin frowned slightly. 'This must have other virtue. And since the episode with Amaryllis' new mantle . . . my lord, I fear there may be graver import to that than we supposed.' She dropped her voice a little, but Amy was sure she heard the words 'Tenth Castle'. She was fascinated and leaned forward to hear more, but Lady Jasmin caught her eye and told her briskly to go and change. 'For your gown reeks of the craglands,' she declared. Amy could smell nothing unusual, but she left obediently. Obviously Lady Jasmin wanted her out of the way.

Sophie came to help her change. To Amy's relief, the tower maid seemed to have put aside her worries, for she smiled and showed Amy the twisted metal ring she had bought from the Bright One's pack. ' 'tis for Jarman,' she said matter-of-factly when Amy admired it. 'A charm to keep him safe on the ocean and bring him home to me.'

'A love potion!' crowed Amy, but Sophie blushed and scolded her.

'Miss, I'd have no dealings with such, and so you know! A lad's love that must be paid for is not worth the coin. Yet a charm from a Bright One—'tis a blessing indeed, and her visit to this castle doubly fortunate.'

'What do you mean?' asked Amy, but Sophie didn't answer. Instead she smiled at Amy and said shyly: 'I wish you could come with us to the Great Fair, Miss.'

'So do I,' said Amy wistfully.

After Sophie had gone, Amy crept up to the coffer attic to have a last look down at the incredible view. She was going home tonight, and she wanted to remember everything—even the unnerving bits like the brush with the sewing dame. When she returned to Amaryllis' chamber, she was considerably surprised to find Crag there, plinking mournfully on a stringed instrument rather like a malnourished guitar. He scowled at her.

'I thought I'd not be looked for here,' he said briefly and gave an odd laugh. 'And have no fear, sister Amaryllis. I'll not tell our lady mother I saw you leave the spiral.'

'I don't mind if you do!' said Amy truthfully. 'But keep playing if you like.'

Crag strummed a chord, high and pure. 'So,' he said his fingers rippling over the strings, 'you have won our lady mother's agreement to your rides about the estate?'

Amy nodded, not quite sure of his mood. 'Tomorrow our lord father will choose a crimson reinbeast for the Fair.'

'A weighty task,' said Crag.

'If it were me, I'd take one of each colour,' said Amy.

The boy looked at her with obvious astonishment. 'Shame, Amaryllis! Even to consider putting the pride of the Fourth Castle to such risk! Misplaced pride, I agree, but surely you do not. That none other may breed the reinbeast is the matter at the very heart of our castle's vainglory!' He looked at her consideringly. 'But perhaps you did not know that to breed reinbeast one needs to have two: male and female?'

Amy blushed. She didn't need Crag Loveday to teach her the facts of life!

'Of *course* I knew!' she snapped.

Crag laughed, and made the instrument laugh too. 'My apologies, wise sister. I shall add only that our lord father—and his forebears—have ever taken care that only male reinbeast leave the craglands. Gelded, they make draught animals and produce excellent fleece, yet a man may never seek to increase his stock by natural means.' He looked at her consideringly. 'But I have thought from our lord father's strictures on my own lack of knowledge of these matters that your understanding was perfection itself?'

Amy felt herself reddening. Crag was being sarcastic and she didn't like that a bit. Almost, she thought she preferred Craig's outright insults to this! 'I know most of it,' she lied, 'but there are just a few things I wasn't clear about. I do see that if they can't breed their own, they have to buy the fleece—or a new animal. Have you seen the lovely gold baby in the stable?'

Crag scowled. 'I have. 'tis an animal, a strange hue, but elsewise like the others.'

He looked so depressed that Amy decided to change the subject. She said at random: 'Make your thingie laugh again.'

Crag cocked an eyebow at her and obliged.

'Can it cry too?'

He played a sobbing note. 'It can also bleat like the cub reinbeast you favour so, and what is this?' He played a leaping, bounding phrase and Amy clapped her hands. 'It's the blue ones jumping down the craglands! Have you done that for Lord Mi—for Lord Father?'

Crag's face went sullen again. 'Our lord father cares not to hear,' he said, and stalked out.

That evening, Amy knelt by the coffer, tempted all over again. She had enjoyed talking with Crag, she had loved the reinbeast, and meeting the Bright One had been a fascinating experience. Then there was Sophie and her sweetheart and dear Red, and . . .

And it was all fascinating, like reading a wonderfully strange book, but better.

'You ought to be ashamed of yourself, Amy Day!' she told herself fiercely. 'What about Amaryllis?'

Deliberately, she pictured Amaryllis as she might be now. White with terror at the sight of a truck, bowled over by a bicycle . . . swallowing a handful of painkillers thinking they were sweets.

And what if the gang had lost patience and come for Amy already? Amy felt sick. It was weak of her to give in to Caz, but to let someone else suffer instead—that was disgusting. Worse than deserting Marina, because Marina had known . . . had, in a way, brought it on herself.

She opened the coffer then closed it hurriedly as Sophie came to do her hair. She must not upset Sophie again. She must go to bed as usual and let the real Amaryllis handle her return as she saw fit. As she'd have to handle her own return, to Caz.

As soon as Sophie had gone, Amy knelt again by the coffer. This time she was less hasty, feeling under piles of clothes rather than flinging them around.

'You'll be happy to see her back, won't you?' she said to Red. 'But oh, I'll miss you . . .' She patted the spellhound and, greatly daring, put her arms around him. Reg would have gone all soppy and started licking her at that, but Red merely rested his fine head on her shoulder so that she felt his strange aura like a tiny vibration through her own body. She sighed, then tossed back a swinging plait and began to search more methodically, lifting out and replacing items as she went.

'Oh, where is it?' she said a few minutes later. 'I know I put it in here.'

She took out everything, and began all over again. But there was no green book in the coffer.

# 12. AMARYLLIS
## *Schizzo*

There was a shock of cold as the water closed over Amaryllis' head. Her foot touched the bottom and she rose slowly. One hand and her head broke the surface, and she had a confused impression of green grass and bare brown legs before she sank once more, water surging into her nose and mouth.

It hurt horribly and she was convinced she was going to die, murdered by the boy who looked like her brother.

When a hand grabbed her painfully by the hair and plucked her to the surface, she clutched at it and kicked out.

'Cut—that—out!' panted Craig, as he towed her to the side of the pool and half hoisted her out of the water.

Amaryllis lay slumped, gasping and choking, trying to shut out Craig's roughly insistent voice. 'What happened, Amy? Amy! Was it cramp! *Amy!*'

A light slap across the cheek forced her to open her

eyes. They stung and watered. Craig shook her. 'What the hell were you playing at, El Creepo? Trying to drown yourself? Anyone'd think you couldn't swim!'

'I cannot,' gasped Amaryllis.

'Don't give me that. You're the little champ, remember!'

Amaryllis said nothing. Craig stared at her, then swung round as his friend came loping back across the grass.

'Hey! What's up?'

'Amy got a mouthful, that's all,' improvised Craig. 'She's OK now, aren't you, Ame?'

'I thought you said she could swim?' said Jason suspiciously. 'Geez—Dad'd kill me if I let some kid drown in his precious pool!'

'Yeah, well I chucked her in, didn't I? Didn't give her time to close her mouth. Sorry, Ame.'

Amaryllis glared at him.

'Coming back in?' said Jason.

'Yeah, come on, you'll be OK up the shallow end,' said Craig, and bundled her back into the water. 'C'mon, give you a race across! And keep your mouth shut.'

He surged off. Amaryllis lost her footing and fell, choking on another mouthful of water. Craig heard, and wallowed back to lift her up again. He stared at her as if she were some strange kind of fish. 'Hey!' he said in a fierce undertone. 'You really *can't* swim, can you?'

Amaryllis glared at him. He had changed his mind about killing her, but how *dare* he play pretence like this?

'You think to make me feared,' she said in a low

shaking voice. 'You think to take my life away. I tell you, you shall not do it, witch's spawn or no!'

She pushed him violently away from her, so angry that she scarcely knew what she said. How *dared* he?

Craig seized her wrist in a casual grip and dragged her to her feet. 'Come on, you! We're going home!' He called curtly over his shoulder to his friend. 'See you later!'

Amaryllis had a confused impression of Jason's gaping face, but Craig marched her out the gate and down the road.

Everyone seemed to be staring as they dripped up the path beside the roadway, and once the girl on a bicycle gawked at Amaryllis and shouted out something unintelligible. Again Amaryllis took no notice of her. She would not show fear and she would not show shame. Anger was the only alternative, and she clung to it fiercely.

Reg had stopped howling and was sniffing mournfully under the fence when they reached home. He uttered a yelp of shock as Craig thrust Amaryllis through the gate, but pressed up to follow them into the house, his eyes flickering uneasily from one to the other.

'Right,' ordered Craig, banging the door shut behind them. 'You're going to tell me what the blazes is going on.'

Amaryllis looked up defiantly. As if he didn't know! But a daughter of the Nine Castles must show courage.

'Naught,' she said deliberately.

Craig's face went an extraordinary colour and his fingers gripped her like claws. 'None of that, Creepface!

There's something weird with you, Amy, and you're going to tell me exactly what it is. Geez! How could you act so stupid in front of Jase? He's the original motor-mouth! Now tell!'

'One who would murder me? I'll tell you naught!'

Craig slapped her face. Not hard, but it stung. Amaryllis shrieked. She had never been struck in her life before she came to this barbaric place. Reg, who had been staring at the pair of them as if his world had gone mad, leapt up with a volley of barks.

'You're mad!' croaked Craig, backing away and almost falling over the dog. 'You've gone schizzo! Geez, Amy!'

Amaryllis put one hand over her cheek and licked her lips, considering possible routes of escape. Craig's face had drained even more, and it suddenly occurred to her that he was just as frightened as she was. Frightened of her. She felt powerful.

'It is you who are mad,' she said slowly. 'You have hurt me and harried me and tried to kill me in the water.'

'No, you've got it wrong!' protested Craig. 'Look—Amy—this is all a game, isn't it? You getting back at me for something?'

Amaryllis made no reply and presently Craig gave a weak laugh. 'Geez, you really had me going for a minute, El Creepo! I thought Ma was right and you'd sprained your brain.'

Amaryllis relaxed. Perhaps after all it was all right.

'Hang on a minute, though,' said Craig suddenly. 'You nearly drowned just now. You wouldn't do that for a joke—not little Amy, the nearest thing to a salmon with two legs.'

Amaryllis shivered. 'I am wet,' she pointed out coldly. 'I wish to dry myself.'

'Wet, hell!' yelled Craig. 'You're lucky you're not *dead*! Hey, that Brandon girl hasn't been giving you pills or anything, has she?'

Amaryllis stared at him uncomprehendingly.

'You been sniffing then? Your voice sounds funny.'

'Sniffing is for hounds,' said Amaryllis.

'You *are* flamin' well schizzo!' roared Craig. 'That's all we need!'

Amaryllis glared at him. It wasn't *he* who'd been roughly transplanted into some crazy world, so why was *he* yelling?

'I am not your sister Amy,' she said. 'I am Lady Amaryllis Loveday. I am a daughter of the Fourth Castle and you have no right to speak like this."

Craig made calming down motions with his hands. 'All right, all right, Amy, don't carry on.'

'Amaryllis!' she snapped.

'Ammyrillus, then. Cripes, where'd you get that one from? Listen, Ammyrillus—er—will you please let me speak to Amy?'

Amaryllis stared at him. How did he expect her to do that? 'If I could speak to your Amy,' she remarked, 'I might be able to get home.'

'Yeah, that's right. Home. Oz, right? The Emerald City? Xanth?' Craig began to back towards the lounge-room door.

'Where are you going?' demanded Amaryllis.

'I'm going to get someone to fix you up,' said Craig soothingly. 'Make you feel better. You're hallucinating or something. Gran can . . .'

'No!' gasped Amaryllis. 'Not the witch!' The colour drained right out of her face and she had a blurred impression of almost identical horror on the faces of Craig and Reg as she dropped.

When she came to her senses, she was on her bed. Craig was hovering close by, almost as white-faced as she. 'Amy?' he said.

She turned her face away.

'Hey, if it's that bad we'll play it your way,' he said mildly. 'You reckon your name's Amaryllis, right?'

She nodded cautiously, the pillow clammy under her neck.

'Well then,' said Craig, still in that unusually gentle voice, 'if you're Amaryllis, where's my sister Amy?'

# 13. Amy

## *Bargain*

my's scalp crept. It was one thing to wish romantically that she could stay, but a cold hard shock to find she had to.

Calm down, she told herself, taking deep, steadying breaths. Books don't vanish. If it was in the coffer before, it must be now.

She searched again, and it wasn't.

So someone must have taken it. For sure, they *talked* about magic here, but she hadn't actually seen any. Except for Red, and perhaps his strangeness was mere wishful thinking . . .

'Red, where is it?' she asked. 'Where's her book?' Red looked at her steadily and she jumped up and stamped her foot. 'I tell you I can't get home without it! Oh—what's the use of you?'

She forced herself to consider who had access to Amaryllis' chamber and also knew of the book. The list was painfully short.

Sophie and Gillie knew she had the book, and Sophie knew where she kept it.

Sophie and Gillie came and went in the chamber. So did Crag and Lady Jasmin, but neither of these two would root about in the coffer.

She'd confront Sophie. Now, or how could she sleep?

Sophie was not in the coffer attic, but Amy heard music and followed it to a room where Crag bent over his lute, playing what seemed to be a fiendishly complicated piece.

'Crag,' she said loudly, 'where does Sophie sleep?'

Crag fumbled a chord, and looked startled, then a mischievous smile lit his face. 'Take care Lady Mother does not hear you asking such information of me, Amaryllis!'

'What?' said Amy blankly. 'Oh, don't be silly, Crag. Sophie's got a boyfriend—Gillie's brother. She's not interested in you even if . . . oh!'

'Then I may safely tell you her chamber is behind the kitchens—as you surely know.'

Amy fled down the spiral stair and through the deserted kitchens, with Red running silently at her side.

Sophie was repairing a torn apron in the room she shared with Gillie, but she put down her needle when Amy burst into the room.

'Miss!' she exclaimed. 'Is something amiss?'

'Yes,' snapped Amy. 'The green book from my coffer. Where is it?'

'Oh, Miss. I—Miss!' said Sophie.

'You *do* know where it is!' pounced Amy. 'Quick, Sophie, where?'

Sophie looked terrified.

'I'm not saying you nicked it,' said Amy impatiently. 'I just want to know where you put it!'

Sophie's face flamed with guilt and Gillie's hand went to her birthchain.

'Just *tell* me!' cried Amy.

'I cannot,' said Sophie.

'What?'

Sophie burst into tears. 'I lodged the witched ledger with the Bright One,' she sobbed. 'For your safety.'

This brought Amy up with a jerk. The Bright One. That strange pedlar woman who had visited the castle. Who had put the wind up Lady Jasmin and captivated Red.

'You gave my book to *her*?' she gasped. 'But *why*? Unless you swapped it for that ring for your boy-friend . . .'

Sophie wept.

'Miss, Miss never think it!' broke in Gillie. 'Indeed, Sophie paid for the ring with her own coin!'

Amy stamped her foot. '*Why* then?'

'I did but seek to protect you from evil influence, Miss,' sobbed Sophie.

'Pro*tect* me!' Amy's voice rose shrilly. 'You stupid girl, you've *stranded* me! If I can't get that book back I'm stuck here forever!'

Both tower maids were weeping now, and from the broken words Gillie kept gasping, Amy realised they were terrified of dismissal.

'Oh, I'm not going to split on you,' she said bitterly. 'That won't bring it back. But what the hell am I going to do? Damn you, stop *crying*!'

'What goes here?' asked someone. Crag was leaning in the arched doorway, looking perplexed.

'Your pardon, Sophie, Gillie,' he told the frightened maids, 'I seek my sister. Ryllis? A word with you.'

'Not *now!*' cried Amy in anguish.

Crag came into the room and took her arm. 'Yes, Ryllis, I think now,' he said. 'Lest you wound a friendship beyond mending.'

Amy let him draw her away. 'I'm sorry, Sophie,' she said stiffly over her shoulder. 'I know you meant to help, but oh, you don't know what you've done!'

Crag marched her up the spiral to her chamber. 'What cause had you to treat Sophie and Gillie so ill?' he asked, letting fall the curtain.

Amy glared at him. 'They gave my book to the Bright One.' She was uncomfortably aware that in Crag's eyes she was fussing about nothing. 'Well,' she said defensively, 'how would you have felt if it had been your lute?'

Crag nodded. 'I see your meaning. But why did they do such a thing?'

'They think it's witched,' said Amy sourly, 'but I've just *got* to have it back!'

Her face must have convinced him, for he said: 'I see. And the Bright One was in the castle today?'

'This morning, but she's gone!' cried Amy. 'She was on her way to a fair.'

'Then she will be fargone by now.'

'Yes,' muttered Amy. 'How can I ever get it back?'

Crag considered. 'I have a plan,' he said at last. 'A bargain to propose. The Bright One goes to the Great

Festival at Western Port, whither I too must go with our lord father.'

Amy nodded.

'Perhaps you recall,' said Crag, 'that a master of music attends the Fair? Master Ash. He seeks an apprentice to train in his craft.'

'So?'

'I would be that apprentice,' said Crag softly. 'Our lady mother will not agree, yet it is *my* life and not hers. If I could take my lute and play for the master . . . I should know my worth.'

'He'd take you on,' said Amy flatly. 'You're good, Crag.'

'Perhaps,' said Crag. 'If he will not, then must I resign myself and do as Lord Father wills.'

'Where do I come in?'

'Mounted, I cannot carry my lute without making show for all,' said Crag. 'Yet if a daughter of the castle should accompany us, she would doubtless ride in the coach with a basket of baggage and her spellhound at her side.' He paused.

'I see,' said Amy slowly. 'You want me to come with you and smuggle your lute in my stuff.'

'I do,' said Crag. 'In return for which I should undertake to seek the Bright One at the Festival and perhaps recover your property.'

Amy digested this offer. 'Will they let me come?'

'I believe so,' said Crag, and his face hardened. 'Your conduct has lately gratified our lady mother. Doubtless Lord Father will plead your case as he will not plead mine.'

'Sophie is going,' warned Amy. 'To meet her boy-friend. Gillie, too.'

Crag misunderstood. 'I would never ask it of a tower maid to carry my lute,' he reproved. 'It would mean her dismissal!'

'It'd mean my hide,' said Amy wryly.

She did wonder briefly—very briefly—whether it was fair to help Crag go against his parents' wishes. But her life—her real life—was at stake. And why shouldn't Crag have his chance to play for this music master? She thought Mike and Jan would have approved. A trade was a good thing to have, and a trade you enjoyed—surely that was a bonus!

'I'll do it,' she said.

Crag bent and kissed her cheek affectionately. 'My strong sister,' he said, and took himself off.

Wowissimo! thought Amy, clasping her cheek. I've actually been kissed!

Then she sighed. Probably it didn't count, since Crag thought he was her brother.

Now the waiting began. Amy prowled restlessly about the castle and grounds. Even the enchanting baby reinbeast could not take her mind from her plight. Besides, she dared not visit it too often: Lady Jasmin must be kept sweet or there'd be no Western Port for Amy.

At night she couldn't sleep. Despite Red's reassuring presence, she lay awake, trying not to blame Sophie for her situation.

If I'd used the book the day I first thought of it, Sophie

couldn't have given it away, she told herself firmly.

And she would have used the book, had it not been for what waited at home. So, really, Caz was to blame, not Sophie, and how Caz would have gloated had she known she was responsible—no matter how indirectly —for stranding Amy Day in someone else's life! But no—Caz would not have gloated. Caz would have looked kindly concerned. Sharon was the one who would have crowed. Or would they? However you looked at it, an Amy stranded in another world was as secure from their machinations as if she'd been—dead.

Amy broke out in a cold sweat and sat up with a jerk. 'Oh God, I'm not dead, am I, Red?' she said aloud.

The spellhound nuzzled her hand and she lay down slowly. 'I don't think much of Heaven, if I am.'

Crag must have begun his campaign immediately, for two mornings later Lady Jasmin called Amy into the Great Chamber and told her she was to attend the Great Fair.

'I have been satisfied with your conduct of late,' she explained. 'You have shown pleasing restraint in movement and in word. In addition, your lord father tells me this is to be an occasion of some historical import: he plans to register the new reinbeast shade at the Fair Hall.'

' 'tis most exciting, Lady Mother,' said Amy demurely.

'Sophie and Gillie make the journey also,' continued Lady Jasmin. 'Sophie's betrothed is to be in port. Although I cannot approve of my tower maids making alliances, I feel that it would be cruel to forbid this meeting—their last for some time.

'That is all. I need hardly say that you, Amaryllis, will remain with Sophie and Gillie or your lord father at all times? Well, Amaryllis? Have you naught to say?'

Amy murmured that she was very grateful.

Sophie did Amy's packing. She was pale, silent and subdued.

'Oh, come on, Sophie,' said Amy at last. 'I'm sorry I yelled at you.'

'Miss, 'twas I at fault,' muttered Sophie.

'Anyway . . .' On the brink of telling Sophie that Crag was going to retrieve her book from the Bright One, caution made Amy change the subject.

'Anyway,' she amended, 'if you don't cheer up, Jarman won't know you.'

Sophie's chin quivered. 'Oh, Miss! 'tis so long since I have seen him . . . and when he has finished his term at sea your lord father promises a position at the castle, and a cottage . . . and we shall wed.'

'How soon?' asked Amy.

'Three seasons more,' said Sophie with a sigh.

'How old will you be?'

Sophie laughed shakily. 'Old enough, Miss, never fear. Fifteen I shall be by that blessed day.' She laid another shift in the wide flat basket. 'There! 'tis done. I will come for you betimes in the morning.'

Crag must have been lurking outside, for he came in as Sophie left. 'My lute,' he said, holding it out.

Amy lifted the top layer of garments and Crag laid

the lute in the basket. Fortunately, it was a slim instrument and took up little room.

'Remember,' she said nervously as she replaced the clothes, 'you've *got* to get that book back! You promised.'

'I shall apply my every effort,' said Crag extravagantly.

Amy left the castle with mixed feelings, unsure whether she would ever return. If she found the book, she thought she should use it immediately and not risk losing it again. Once was bad luck, twice would be criminal carelessness!

But—she did wonder what would happen if she wrote her way home from Western Port. Would she wake far from home?

Amy shrugged. She'd deal with that if it happened. It wasn't too daunting a problem. The prospect of having to get home from—Adelaide, say—was far less problematical than the idea of never getting home at all.

Lord Michael's party was quite large, for a number of villagers had elected to travel with them in convoy. Amy, Sophie, Gillie and the spellhound travelled in a coach: no fairytale conveyance, but a stolid vehicle with a deep well beneath for storing luggage. It was drawn by two of the mighty draught reinbeast and driven by a startlingly handsome but silent young man named Thomas.

Lord Michael and Crag rode ahead, leading the crimson reinbeast chosen for display at the fair.

The coach was not comfortable.

It rumbled along the rough road that ran westward through the estate, seeming to magnify every jolt and rut as it went. Amy was unable to find a comfortable position, and Red, at her feet, seemed equally out of sorts, shifting his paws uneasily as the vehicle swayed.

Sophie showed no surprise when Silent Thomas turned and jerked his head and Gillie moved forward to sit beside him, remaining even after Lord Michael had circled back to warn of an obstruction in the road.

'Doesn't he mind?' asked Amy, lowering her voice.

'Mind?' said Sophie blankly.

Amy gestured circumspectly. 'Them.'

'Miss, Gillie and Thomas have been promised this long time!' laughed Sophie. 'Your lord father is not one to wave back the tide.'

'Oh,' said Amy.

Unless I get home soon, she thought, I'm going to be caught out with something I couldn't possibly have forgotten.

Evening was coming on when they arrived at the outskirts of Western Port. There was plenty of evidence of the Great Fair: ships in the harbour, stalls setting up all around. The narrow streets teemed with brightly dressed people, and Amy saw a handful of draughtbeasts drawing vehicles.

She was daunted. There must be thousands here. How would Crag find Jadetha among so many?

She was so tired that tears began to prick at the back of her nose. Her quest was impossible, even if she could depend on Crag. And could she? Perhaps his assurance had been merely to win her over in the matter of the lute. He couldn't know how important the green ledger was to her—and to his sister Amaryllis.

The smell of fish and unwashed wool mingled with that of spices and leather as the coach trundled and lurched through the ruts. 'And how does my Ryllis like her first sight of Western Port?' asked Lord Michael, bringing his reinbeast alongside the coach.

Amy gritted her teeth. 'Greatissimo!' she muttered. 'It appears very busy, Lord Father,' she said primly.

Lord Michael raised his eyebrows. 'What, no transports? No cries of delight?'

'My back aches,' explained Amy truthfully.

'So,' said Crag, 'does mine.' He slid stiffly from his beast and led the way down the street. 'Shall we go immediately to the inn?' he asked over his shoulder.

Lord Michael agreed, but said he would join them only after he had taken the crimson reinbeast to its quarters at the Nine Castles Pavilion and assured himself of its comfort.

The inn was square and low and made of stone. Crag helped Amy and the tower maids down from the coach. 'Wait,' he whispered in Amy's ear as Sophie and Gillie went into the inn. 'We lie two nights here, for on the morrow the fair proper begins. This eve I shall play for the master. Should he accept me I shall return to the inn and say naught. After sundown on the morrow Lord Father will be busy in the Council of Nine, and I shall then leave this place with the master.'

'What about my book?' put in Amy anxiously.

'On the morrow,' said Crag.

'It's very important.'

'This ledger: *is* it witched that you must find it?' he asked abruptly.

'Oh, not you too!' cried Amy. 'Surely *you* don't believe that rubbish!'

'A man is a simpleton to believe all,' said Crag with dignity. 'Yet he lies in direst peril if he believes naught.' His fingers played with the birthchain on his wrist.

'I must find it!' said Amy again. 'Promise, Crag!'

'I shall do my best.' Crag sounded impatient, and she was afraid to press him further.

# 14. AMARYLLIS
## *Ammo*

maryllis stared suspiciously at Craig.
Did he really believe her, or was this some trick to put her off guard? 'I am not certain,' she said cautiously. 'Perhaps she is at the castle, taking my place as I have taken hers.'

'Yeah, I suppose that's got a sort of screwy logic,' said Craig. He sat down on the foot of the bed. 'All right then, how do we get to this castle? Catch a plane? Say "Abracadabra"? Follow the yellow brick road?'

Amaryllis looked at him disdainfully. 'If I knew how to return I would do so,' she said. 'I must alert my lord father.'

Craig rubbed his chin. 'You must have got here somehow.'

She said nothing.

'You see,' said Craig quite gently, 'that's the weak part of your story. That and the fact that you look just like you've always done.'

'But I do not,' said Amaryllis.

'No?'

'My hair,' she explained, touching it. The short locks were wild but almost dry. 'My own hair is long, and of a brighter hue. This is shorn like that of a fever case, although I have no fever.'

Craig looked bewildered. 'So, according to you, my sister Amy, where she is now, has got hair down to here.' He touched his back.

'Farther,' said Amaryllis with a sigh.

'And does she let it down for the witch to climb up? Well I'm sorry, but I don't buy that.' Craig got up and walked over to the window. 'You've been reading too many fairy tales, Scrawny. What you're on about is a sort of mind transplant, right? Your body—her brain. Or is it your brain—her body? Or both? Whatever it is, I don't buy it—except . . .' He turned round and regarded her thoughtfully.

'Well?' said Amaryllis.

'Except that you nearly drowned,' said Craig, 'and my sister Amy is so scrawny she hardly displaces any water, so she can swim like an eel. And then there's old Reg, who's usually all over you like a rash. Just lately he seems to think you're public enemy number forty-two—although that could be because he reckons you've gone loony tunes. But even being loony tunes shouldn't make you forget how to swim . . . Right, Ammo, explain. Why can't you swim?'

Amaryllis pictured the bleak sea below the Fourth Castle. The rocks that stuck up like fangs, the cold swirling currents. Only the Lords and Masters of the

Third Castle dared to challenge the ocean, and they in ships. She shook her head.

'Well, what *can* you do?' persisted Craig. 'Draw pictures? Sing songs?'

Amaryllis shook her head. 'My brother has music in his mind, not I.'

'Figures. Amy can't sing either. About all she's any good at is swimming—and writing stuff, I suppose. What *do* you do in this place of yours? Marry princes? Fight monsters? Ride dragons?'

'One may not ride a dragon: it is a creature of myth,' said Amaryllis. 'You make game of me. I ride the blue reinbeast when I may. When Lady Mother permits.'

Even now she felt the sullen surge of injustice at the thought. Had she been a son, she would have had her own beast—perhaps a dainty crimson—by now. Instead she was confined to the lady-seat on the heavy-limbed dependable blue.

'Blue reindeer! Geez, you can think 'em up!' said Craig. 'I s'pose I'll have to get hold of Mum or Dad. They'll take you to the head shrinker.' He glanced at his timepiece. 'Dad'll be on the road about now—God knows where Mum's got to, and you don't want Gran and her doses of salts. Tell me about this castle.'

Amaryllis, to keep him calm, told Craig about the castle and her parents, her brother Crag, Sophie and Red. She told him of Master Greenhaven, whom she loved. 'For he allows me some intelligence,' she explained.

At the end of it all she felt she had spoken more words to this Craig than she had said to her own brother in a season or more. But Crag never wanted to speak with her, for all he wished was music, and she had none of that.

They both jumped when Jan and Mike came noisily into the kitchen beyond.

'You there, kids?' called Jan. 'We've brought chicken and chips!'

'Coming!' yelled Craig. Then he dropped his voice and hissed at Amaryllis. 'All right, Ammo. Convince me. I'll keep my mouth shut for a week, then I talk.'

'You will help me?'

He nodded. 'Geez beez, need my head read for doing it though.'

She still didn't trust him, but it was the best she could hope for.

Amaryllis went very warily indeed the next day, but it seemed that Craig was keeping his promise. He watched her more than was comfortable, but he no longer seemed so hostile. Sometimes he came and asked her questions about her life and home. She answered these willingly enough: it seemed to have become as important now that he should know her for who she was than it had previously been that he shouldn't.

Some of the questions did not make sense. For example, he quite frequently referred to someone called 'Caz', asking Amaryllis what had gone wrong, why she and that person were no longer friends.

Amaryllis stared at him blankly when he did this, aware that he was trying to trick her into some answer, some admission which would prove that she was really his sister Amy.

He had quite a few theories and Amaryllis often wished he had something more to do than think up tests for her. Her brother Crag, who was this boy's virtual double in age as well as appearance, was always occupied, either reluctantly learning the business of the estate from Lord Michael or doggedly practising his lute.

'You know what I reckon, Ammo?' Craig said on Friday morning when he managed to corner her out on the porch.

'You have told me enough of what you reckon,' said Amaryllis with a sigh.

Jan opened the window. 'Everything OK out there, kids?'

'Yeah, sure!' answered Craig. Then, to Amaryllis: 'Just like our mum, isn't it? Keeps on about us fighting and now she's got herself in a twist because we're not.'

'She is your mother and not mine,' said Amaryllis.

'Aw, come on.' Craig settled himself beside her. 'Look, what I think is this fight with your mate Caz is worse than you let on. Geez, I've seen her at school, remember!

'I reckon you've got yourself all in a twist about her and you've just opted out, forgotten, made yourself into somebody else.'

Amaryllis sprang up. 'Craig, I do not know this Caz. I have forgotten nothing!'

'OK, OK!' Craig made fending-off motions with his hands and backed off. 'You're Ammo of the castle, and I'm the Good Magician!'

But still he watched her.

# 15. Amy

## Great Fair

he Overdame of the inn did not approve of Amy's association with the tower maids. Nor did she like Red.

It had occurred to Amy to wonder why the very correct Lady Jasmin would allow her daughter to spend the night at an inn. Her question was answered in the sharp grey person of the Overdame, a sort of house mother, who kept autocratic watch over all unmarried girls at the inn. She was far haughtier than Lady Jasmin and she tried to insist that Amy be quartered alone and grandly, and that the spellhound should reside in the stables behind the inn.

'Lady Mother bade me stay with Sophie and Gillie,' persisted Amy. '*And* to keep Red with me.'

'Association with such ill-befits a daughter of the Nine Castles,' pronounced the Overdame.

''tis so, Dame,' put in Sophie anxiously. 'But the Lady Jasmin did indeed bid us stay together . . . enquire of

Miss Loveday's lord father if that is not so! And the hound is a spellhound, well conducted, and of great value.'

The Overdame looked doubtful, and Amy could scarcely blame her. Red had apparently not yet recovered from the discomfort of the coach, for he was whimpering a little and shifting his paws about. Amy patted him, and hoped he'd settle soon.

Fortunately, Lord Michael arrived shortly afterwards. The Overdame interviewed him at length, but she would not allow him over the threshold of the Maidens' Quarters. Negotiations had to be carried out through the quarter-opened doorway.

'Sophie and Gillie are excellent girls, and I trust them as I trust my daughter,' soothed Lord Michael. 'However, if you doubt your ability to watch over Amaryllis, she will naturally stay in the general quarters with me and I shall . . .'

He was not allowed to finish his sentence, for the Overdame exploded with outrage at the idea. Still scolding vigorously, she hustled Lord Michael away. 'Until tomorrow, Ryllis!' he called cheerfully as he departed.

The Maidens' Quarters was practically a prison, but the food was good and the beds soft. When they retired, Sophie (jittering with anticipation for tomorrow) helped Amy as she had at the castle. Apart from that, they might have been three friends. No—thought Amy soberly— they *were* three friends. Girls like Sophie and Gillie were worth fifty of Sharon and Caz.

Later, lying in the dark, she stroked Red's soft ears

and listened to the distant uproar of voices coming from the general quarters of the inn. Gusts of laughter and boisterous conversation ebbed and flowed, and after a while somebody began to play a ballad.

I wonder if that's Crag? thought Amy drowsily, and jerked awake.

It couldn't possibly be Crag, because she still had his lute in her basket. Why hadn't the stupid boy come to fetch it?

But that was obvious. The Overdame would never have allowed him past the door. If Lord Michael had been barred, there was no way that zealous guardian of maidenhood would allow a boy—well, really a young man—to enter her domain.

Well, he should have thought of that, shouldn't he? thought Amy. Then she giggled. This was supposed to be Amaryllis' first journey to Western Port, so probably Crag had never met the Overdame! He didn't strike her as the type to hang around the Maidens' Quarters . . .

But this was serious. If she didn't get his lute to him, perhaps he wouldn't keep his part of the bargain.

The others were asleep, so Amy got out of bed and crept across to the door. Red whimpered, and she hushed him quickly and tried the latch. As she had expected, the door was barred. So was the only outer window, but as she gazed out, a vaguely familiar figure went past in the light of the lamps suspended along the eaves.

It was Silent Thomas, who had driven the coach. Gillie's sweetheart. She recognised his halting step.

'Thomas!' she hissed.

Thomas' feet stuttered on the path and he looked around wildly.

'Up here!'

Amy waved her arm, and Thomas finally looked up. 'Gillie?' he called hopefully. 'My Gillie?'

'No, it's me,' said Amy, feeling foolish. 'Me—Amy—Amaryllis Loveday, I mean.'

'Miss! You must not . . .' Thomas' voice ran up and cracked with outrage. Amy giggled nervously. Whatever was Thomas thinking?

'Thomas, I've got to see Crag. I have something of his.'

Thomas looked very relieved. He nodded, and disappeared.

Amy choked. Had poor Thomas really thought she was flirting with him?

After a time she began to shiver. She wanted to go back to bed. What if the Overdame caught her hanging about the window like this? She'd suspect the worst.

Then someone was standing under the window. 'Ryllis! Amaryllis! Are you there?'

Crag.

'Yes!' she whispered. 'Wait!' She fumbled for her basket and extracted the lute. Turning the instrument sideways, she slid it carefully between the window bars. Holding the end of the bridge, she stretched her arm to its fullest extent, her forehead and shoulder pressing uncomfortably against the bars.

Crag reached up, and after an age his hand touched the lute, grasped, and brought it down. He ran his fingers over the wood as if it were a much-loved pet.

'Don't forget,' she hissed. 'The Bright One. Jadetha of the Seventh Castle. You must find her, first chance you get.'

She thought Crag nodded.

'I hope the master likes your playing!' she whispered.

She couldn't see his face, but his quiet words drifted up. 'If he does, we each get our heart's desire, do we not, Amaryllis?'

Amy clung to the bars. 'How?' she whispered. Did Crag know?

Crag chuckled. 'If I am gone as a minstrel, dear sister, it is surely you who must one day be Lord of the Fourth Castle!'

A cluster of flaming torches appeared along the path and Amy stepped back out of range of the light. When she returned to the window, the boy who was not her brother had gone.

Tomorrow, she thought. Tomorrow.

Sophie would see her sweetheart tomorrow, Crag would go with the master, Lord Michael would register the golden reinbeast, and she—she would find the Bright One with Crag's help, get back Amaryllis' book and finally go home.

Breakfast was hurried in the morning, for the Great Fair was beginning and everyone was eager to reach the market circle.

'Miss,' protested Sophie as Amy tried to peer through the window. 'Do be still! I cannot weave the braid. And see? You're fidgeting the spellhound!'

Sophie was nervous too. Her capable hands shook as

she brushed Amy's hair. 'Now put on your new mantle and we shall see how it sets—there, 'tis perfect!' Sophie sighed with relief, for it had been she who had finally finished stitching the blue reinbeast-weave mantle.

Lord Michael met them at the foot of the stairs, with Crag and Silent Thomas standing a pace or two behind. Crag looked sullen.

'What happened?' mouthed Amy.

Crag shook his head at her.

'Now,' said Lord Michael, 'let us go. Thomas, you will please escort Gillie and Sophie to the "Lady Trinity" and wait with them until Jarman shall come. Or wait—perhaps you should remain with them the full day, so as to escort the girls back safe to the inn. I trust that will be no hardship?'

Silent Thomas blushed and grinned.

'Crag, you will come with me to the Fair Hall. We have great tidings to register there.'

'What about me?' asked Amy.

The Lord Michael smiled at her. 'You shall come with your brother and myself to share our triumph, for 'tis yours as well.' He turned to Thomas and the maids. 'Fare well, and return when you will.'

'And what,' said Crag thoughtfully, as the three moved away, 'would my lady mother say to that?'

Amy could guess what Lady Jasmin would say, but Lady Jasmin would never know. Lord Michael was much more relaxed about everything.

'Well?' she demanded, as she and Red fell in beside Crag.

'Well?' mocked Crag, offering his arm.

Amy took it in what she hoped was a blasé fashion. 'What happened? Did you meet with the master?'

Crag looked at her coolly. 'I did so, but he would not hear me play. He bade me attend him at sundown at his inn, when he will hear us all.'

'All?'

'It seems I am not the only one wishful of this honour.'

'Will you help me look for my book now then?' said Amy.

'Indeed,' agreed Crag, 'but come, we must not fall behind. What ails the hound?'

'I don't quite know,' said Amy. 'Perhaps he doesn't like Western Port.'

Crag looked about. 'To be sure, the air is thick with intrigue and thievery,' he said. 'No doubt he senses it, and it plays on his nerves.'

'That must be it,' said Amy with relief. 'He's been making me quite jumpy. Come on, Red, you can't look after everybody.'

They hurried to catch up with Lord Michael.

On the way to the Fair Hall, they passed rows of stalls and pavilions. Amy peered anxiously at the proprietors, but although many wore colourful clothes, she never saw the Bright One. The thing was obviously impossible, like looking at Melbourne Show for a person you had met once and whose interests you did not know.

The Fair Hall was a vast building of most peculiar design.

'It's all lumpy!' said Amy, rousing herself from her despondency.

Lord Michael chuckled. 'I must speak with Master

AMY AMARYLLIS

Greenhaven when he returns from the north! Has he
neglected to tell you of the Nine Castles and their
emblems?'

Amy wondered who Master Greenhaven might be,
but prudently didn't ask.

'Then Crag will enlighten you,' said Crag's father.

'The hall is nine-sided,' recited Crag in a sing song
tone, 'to reflect the great Nine Castles of the land.

'The First Castle, being of caves, holds the ancient
rights to the spiderlace and its secret design. Its emblem
then is the bobbin.

'The Second Castle, being of forests, holds the ancient
rights to the cofferwood. Its emblem then is the great
tree.

'The Third Castle, being of water, holds the ancient
rights to the ships and the sea. Its emblem then is the
ship.

'The Fourth Castle, being of crags, holds the ancient
rights of the reinbeast weave. Its emblem then is the
golden reinbeast.

'The Fifth Castle, being of earth, holds the ancient
rights to the stargem mines of the west. Its emblem then
is the stargem.

'The Sixth Castle, being of plains, holds the ancient
rights to the grasslands and medical herbs. Its emblem
then is the bright garland.

'The Seventh Castle, being of byways, holds the
ancient rights to the magic of words and ways. Its
emblem then is the green and endless circle.

'The Eighth . . .'

'Enough!' said Lord Michael. 'I need not chide Master

Greenhaven on my son's account! But come, we must reach the registry.'

Amy followed him into the Fair Hall, which was crowded with richly dressed people. A flock of grey-clad, grey-faced men with stargems at their belts bowed distantly to Lord Michael and more deeply to Amy and Crag.

'The Fifth Castle, and your kinsmen,' said Lord Michael in a low voice. He sighed very softly and rolled his eyes. 'Alas, they would speak with me of rabble lords and insu*rrrr*ection!' He turned courteously to the greyest of the grey ones.

As he did so, a group of fluttering butterfly robes passed near the entrance of the hall. Those around them fell back, with hands flying nervously to the chains around their throats and wrists.

'The Bright One!' exclaimed Amy, but neither Crag nor Lord Michael had noticed. Jittering with suspense, she tugged at Crag's arm.

'Over there! Quick, we've got to catch her!' She pointed, but the butterfly people had gone. 'Oh, quick— they've gone!' She began to push her way through the crowds, tripping over the spellhound in her haste. He gave an uneasy yelp.

'Ryllis! Wait!' called Crag, and she felt his hand on her elbow. He gave her a little shake. 'You must wait here! The hound warns of danger. Stay, return to Lord Father. I shall find this Bright One.'

'Well go on then!' cried Amy, mad with impatience. 'Stop her, quickly!'

Crag bit his lip, seeming curiously reluctant. 'Go to

Lord Father,' he repeated, giving her a push in Lord Michael's direction. He turned away, clasping his left wrist in his right hand, plunging through the crowd. Amy stared after him, then dived in pursuit, the spellhound padding beside her and uttering little yelps of distress.

By the time she reached the doorway, Crag and the brightly garbed strangers had disappeared into the swarming crowd.

'No!' Amy wailed, thumping her fist into her palm in anguish. She peered about, but the Great Fair seethed with people, and any one of the myriad voices she heard could have been Crag's.

Several people looked at her curiously, and she became aware that she was the only girl to be standing alone. Everyone else had escorts: fathers, husbands, brothers, sweethearts, sons. She lifted her chin and caught sight of a thin plain woman with jet-bead eyes and a puckered mouth. It looked like the woman who had been, so briefly, sewing dame to Lady Jasmin. Who had tried to put—something—in the hem of the blue mantle. But this person was finely dressed, her hair built in an elaborate style. Gold rings glittered from her ears and . . . but it *was* the same woman. Amy was abruptly certain. And the sewing dame had seen her, and was coming swiftly towards her.

Beside her, Red's hackles rose and he snarled. The woman paused for an instant, then her pursed mouth opened and she made a flinging motion with one hand. The spellhound yelped. The hand darted again. Amy tried to back away, but she was hemmed in by a press of people near the door. Yet the sewing dame seemed to have no problems. People melted away from her path. 'Miss Amaryllis Loveday, is it not?' said the sewing dame affably. 'In her fine new mantle. Trimmed with stargems, I see!'

Red surged forward as if to attack, but the sewing dame gave a sharp yap of laughter and snapped her hands together above the spellhound's head. It was a strangely hollow, echoing sound, like a hammer striking rock under water, and Red shook his head in obvious distress.

'Stargems,' said the woman again. 'Not suitable for a child. And yet perhaps a child may have its uses . . .'

Don't be stupid, Amy told herself frantically. She can't do anything to you. It's broad daylight and there are like a thousand people here! She looked swiftly about for Crag. Or Lord Michael. Or the Overdame. Anyone. But the eye she caught belonged to a tall young man in a glimmering cloak. He stepped forward, and bowed.

'Good morning, Miss Loveday,' he said politely. 'May I be of service?'

Amy suddenly realised how terrified she had been. 'Yes, sir, this woman . . .' She indicated the sewing dame, but the jet-eyed woman was no longer there. Yet she must be somewhere close, for Red was still broadcasting his distress. 'A woman in a dark dress,' she said quickly. 'She had black eyes and a funny mouth and . . .'

'I saw her, Miss Amaryllis,' said the young man cheerfully. 'And I think you had best not have much to do with the likes of that one.'

'I don't think so either,' agreed Amy. She smiled, tentatively, and patted Red. She had no idea who this young man was, but he evidently knew her, or rather Amaryllis. Then suddenly it came to her that he was wearing reinbeast weave. Perhaps he was a relation? Or had been a member of Lord Michael's party?

'Are we kinsmen, sir?' she hazarded, trying to look shy rather than desperate.

The man laughed. 'To a distant degree, Miss Amaryllis.'

'I thought we must be,' she said, indicating his cloak. 'You wear reinbeast weave.'

He bowed again. 'Lord Random, at your command.'

'Of the Fourth Castle?' she asked, trying to sound knowledgeable. (Where was Crag?)

He laughed again, a curiously unamused sound. 'I cannot claim that honour yet. Shall we say, rather, of a new castle?'

Amy's mind raced. There were only nine castles, surely, but—an extraordinary thought popped into her head. Could this man possibly be betrothed to Amaryllis Loveday? These people certainly married early—look at Sophie! And presumably if a man were not of the Nine Castles yet married into one of them, he became part of that line. Or formed a new one? Unless it worked the other way round and the woman took *his* rank . . . and they both became commoners.

She glanced about. 'I am waiting for my brother,' she offered. 'He will be coming soon.' Red barked as if to agree.

'Ah, yes, young Crag of the Lute—does he still aspire to be a minstrel?'

Amy spread her hands and smiled, her mind working

furiously. This man seemed to know a great deal about the Lovedays. A close family friend? More than that? 'Quiet, Red,' she said sternly as the spellhound yipped once more. 'The woman can't get at us now.'

But Lord Random was speaking again, offering his services as company until Crag returned.

Amy couldn't quite see how she could stop him, and anyway, what harm could there be in standing beside a family friend in broad daylight? It certainly felt safer than standing alone at the mercy of the sewing dame—whoever or whatever she really was. Amy shivered.

'And who of the Fourth Castle, besides yourself and your brother, honours the Fair this season?' asked Lord Random.

'Lord Father is here,' said Amy.

'Doubtless to attend the Council of Nine at sundown?'

She nodded.

'And shall we common folk have the pleasure of casting for reinbeast this time?'

'We have brought along a crimson,' said Amy proudly.

'A crimson! Then I shall certainly cast, and often, and bless the tile at each throw!' said Lord Random with satisfaction. He lifted the edge of his cloak. 'As you see, my only beast is of the poorest blue shade. A crimson would be a prize indeed for myself—and my lady! But tell me, Miss Amaryllis, how does Lord Michael progress in his quest for the lost shades? A simpleton's errand, some do say, but I am not one of them. I have the greatest respect for Lord Michael Loveday when it comes to husbanding the reinbeast.'

Amy wished he'd stop talking, but after all, it was no secret. 'Lord Father,' she said with vicarious pride, 'registers a new shade today.'

Lord Random displayed all the delight that Crag had not.

'What a triumph!' he said warmly. 'Can it be of rose, lost many seasons since?'

Amy shook her head. 'Gold,' she said. And then, to her intense relief, she saw Crag pushing his way back towards the hall. 'And here is my brother.'

Lord Random nodded. 'Then I shall leave you to his care,' he said gracefully, and turned away.

Amy forgot him. 'Well?' she demanded as Crag approached. 'Did you catch up with her? Where's the book?'

It struck her that Crag looked rather green in the face, but she was too impatient to worry about that.

'The Bright One Jadetha was not of that company,' said Crag shortly. 'One said, however, that she would meet with you after sundown.'

'Where?' asked Amy eagerly. 'Will she come to the inn?'

Crag gave her a strange look. 'One does not seek to command those of the Seventh Castle. She will meet you at the Bright Pavilion.'

'But where is it? How shall I find my way? Oh—I hope that sewing dame has left by then.'

'Amaryllis,' said Crag firmly. 'I know not of what you babble, but you shall not need to find your way, for naturally I shall escort you.'

# 16. AMARYLLIS
## *Grandam*

The time Craig had given her was passing swiftly and Amaryllis was still no closer to going home. Every morning she opened her eyes with a sense of resignation: she was still in the world they called 'Australia'.

If this goes on, she thought, I shall begin to wonder if Craig is not right and if I am not truly his sister under some witchment. Perhaps that is what the enemy intends!

This idea frightened her so much that she finally made the decision she had been putting off. She would visit the witch, Craig's grandam.

The thought made her quake inwardly, but it was the only thing to do. She would go to the witch and confess her situation. She would hurl herself on the witch's mercy and beg for her help.

Amaryllis went to Craig. 'Where shall I find the grandam?' she asked.

'At home, unless she's out gassing to her mates at the bowls club,' said Craig. 'Why?'

'Will you take me to her?' asked Amaryllis. 'I have a favour to beg.'

'Geez, there's a turn-up for the flamin' books! You've spent the whole holidays so far making excuses *not* to go to Gran's place! OK, OK, spare me the Ammo-of-the-castle routine. I'll take you after dinner.'

I must plan, she thought. She had no gift to offer the witch, and no birthchain to keep her safe. The dog Reg was no spellhound, so all she would have to rely upon was her own courage, the dubious support of Craig and—perhaps—the goodwill of the witch who would surely wish her own kinswoman home.

The telephone rang just as they were leaving.

'For you, Craig!' called Jan.

'Hang on a minute,' said Craig to Amaryllis, and he went back into the house. He was gone quite a while, and Amaryllis felt her apprehension building. Then he came out, hurdled the porch rail and headed for the garden shed at the run, a fringed towel draped around his neck. When he emerged from the shed he was wheeling the machine he called his '10 Speed'. He paused briefly beside Amaryllis to buckle on his helmet.

'Craig, I cannot travel on that!' she reminded him. 'It is a conveyance for one.'

'What?' Craig wrinkled his forehead for a moment. 'Oh, Amy—look, there's been a change of plan. You'll have to go to Gran's by yourself.'

'You pledged to escort me,' reminded Amaryllis.

'Yeah, but that was Jase on the blower: they're having

water polo tryouts at the pool! The dork forgot to tell me the other day. Gotta go—you can get yourself over to Gran.'

'I cannot!' wailed Amaryllis.

'Sure you can. Look.' Craig got her by the elbow. 'You go down this street to the green house, see, then you turn right and walk along to the bowls club. Got that? Of course you have! Gran's place is in Severne Crescent, right at the end. Geez, you could find your way there blindfolded! Stay with Gran and I'll call in for you after the tryouts. OK? See ya!'

Throwing his leg over the bar, Craig launched himself and his machine down the street. Amaryllis looked after him in dismay. She could have put off this journey for another day, but she knew down in her soul that on another day she might not have the courage to do it. Perhaps the red hound would consent to accompany her? But even though she cajoled him, he hesitated, and then Jan called and he bounded back towards the house with evident relief. Amaryllis sighed and set out alone.

More than ever she wished she had some offering for the witch. She put her hand doubtfully to her throat. The fine silver chain she had broken on the first morning had been mended and returned to her. Clearly it represented some charm or other, but it could not have been a strong one, else Jan would have been more concerned at its absence.

She walked stolidly, trusting to luck that she was going the right way, turning right past the green house. She didn't know what a bowls club might be, so she concentrated on looking for Severne Crescent (a most portentous name and sure proof of witchery—had she needed more!). Before she could find it, she met the grandam herself, garbed all in white and grasping a strange limp basket. Amaryllis didn't think much of the weaver who had fashioned that: the mesh was loose and ill-made.

'Amy, love!' cried the grandam, flinging her arms about Amaryllis.

The swinging basket whipped about and curled itself round Amaryllis' legs, making her squeak with surprise.

'About time you dropped in on your old gran!' said the grandam happily. 'I was starting to think you'd given up on me as well as your mate Caz.'

'Your pardon.' Amaryllis backed nervously away, but the grandam swept on.

'Only thing is, you've caught me on the hop—just got back from bowls, spitting chips, dying for a cuppa, and blow me if I'm not out of milk! Always the way. Tell you what, Amy, you go ahead and put the jug on to boil, eh? Key's under the mat.'

Amaryllis found herself standing in the middle of the road while the grandam bustled away.

Curious indeed, thought Amaryllis. Does she not recognise me for a changeling? She was tempted to retreat, but she had not come so far to turn back now, so she raised her chin and went on.

'Hey you!' called an abrupt voice behind her. Amaryllis turned about. It was the fair girl, the one on the bicycle. Amaryllis wished to have nothing to do with that one, but the machine swerved to a halt across her path.

'You!' said the girl. Her eyes were unfriendly beneath her helmet.

'Are you speaking to me?' enquired Amaryllis. Unconsciously she put back her shoulders and raised her chin. She was not Lady Jasmin's daughter for nothing.

'Yer right I am!' The girl glowered at her, seeing not a daughter of the Fourth Castle but plain Amy Day, whom she had known since they were both five years old.

'I do not know you,' said Amaryllis. She stepped around the bicycle and kept on walking.

'Hey!' yelled the girl. 'You looking for trouble, Day? Caz is after you!' Her voice became sarcastic. 'Remember Caz? Your friend Caz?'

She circled in front of Amaryllis again.

'This Caz is no friend of mine,' said Amaryllis truthfully. 'I do not know her.'

The girl sniggered. 'You wish! Don't say I didn't warn you, Day, that's all. Today's the day, Day, and you'll meet us at the Mall at two—or else!'

She swooped off down the street, leaving Amaryllis staring after her in perplexity. How could such an ill-bred person be a friend of Amaryllis' double?

It was nothing to do with her, she thought, and dismissed it from her mind with a shrug.

# 17. AMY
## *Betrayal*

ord Michael returned from registering the golden reinbeast in a great good humour, which Amy hesitated to break by mentioning her brush with the sewing dame. And, besides, it had come to nothing. Lord Random had saved her and Red seemed to have recovered from whatever the woman had done to him.

'Come,' said Lord Michael, offering an arm to Amy. 'The casting has started—'tis time to see what luck attends our crimson.'

Crag scowled.

Lord Michael took them through a covered way to emblem banners which marked out the Nine Castles Pavilion. The noise was incredible there, for thousands of people jostled and milled to examine the prizes on display. One facet of the pavilion held a casket set with a single enormous stargem. In another was arranged a length of the finest lace Amy had ever seen.

'Spiderlace,' said Lord Michael. 'Shall we cast for your lady mother?'

He paid a heavy coin to the attendant and signed his name on a small tile, which was dropped into a slit-topped casket.

Every facet of the pavilion held just one item, obviously of high prestige, representing the concerns of the Nine Castles.

Some, whose lots were intangible, used symbolic representations. A voyage to a far land, eagerly sought by the younger men, was shown by the emblem of the Third Castle: a tiny model ship.

'And here is our own lot,' said Lord Michael. Amy peered through the crowd. The crimson reinbeast was penned in a stall. It looked curious, but not at all afraid: it was a friendly creature and bleated hopefully at members of the crowd as they passed.

'How goes it?' Lord Michael asked the beast's attendant, one of those who had ridden from the village. The man grinned and waggled his fingers. Evidently it went well.

'Shall we cast for the reinbeast?' asked someone directly behind Amy.

'A gelt buck once again,' muttered the man's companion. 'The Fourth Lord takes no chances.'

'He is no such fool,' said the first, and laughed. 'The buck is a taking animal: I shall cast.'

Once Amy thought she saw Lord Random in conversation with a man in a blue robe, but when she looked again he was gone. She wondered if he had cast for the reinbeast. He had sounded eager to do so outside the Fair Hall . . . Her eyes moved restlessly on, but she never saw the sewing dame—or the Bright One. And after Crag's message she could hardly ask him to search again.

The day passed slowly. Lord Michael was indulgent and let Amy see whatever took her eye. They ate strange things and saw stranger: once Crag came to a sudden halt and gazed worshipfully through the crowd to where a man, slight and fair, tried the tone of a lute. 'The master!' he told Amy in a low voice.

Amy was surprised at the man's youth, but her attention was distracted then by a glimpse of Sophie, arm in arm with her sweetheart. Gillie's brother was not handsome, but he had curly hair and a laughing face. Just the thing for Sophie, Amy thought. She needed someone lighthearted.

She wondered if Jarman was wearing his twisted ring, but even this could not occupy her mind for long.

Would sundown never come?

At last the sun did decline and, although the Great Fair showed no signs of rest, Lord Michael turned back toward the inn. 'I think you must miss the meeting of the Nine Castles, my Ryllis,' he said cheerfully. 'To tell the truth, I would I could miss it as well! It is apt to be long and of great boredom. My colleagues would wear their castles upon their backs like snails, were they able—except perhaps for Lord Lucien, whose interests are otherwise.' Lord Michael touched his birthchain at the thought. He turned to Crag. 'But you, my son—you will accompany me?'

Crag yawned. 'I think not, Lord Father. I am weary and we must ride on the morrow.'

Lord Michael shrugged philosophically. 'Then you may escort your sister to the inn and deliver her safe to the Maidens' Quarters. Have a care the she-dragon Overdame does not eat you!'

'I shall,' said Crag shortly, and he offered his arm to Amy.

Lord Michael nodded, turned on his heel and strode away in the direction of the Fair Hall. Amy watched him out of sight. She had grown fond of Lord Michael, and if all went well she would not see him again.

'Come,' said Crag. 'We must hurry.'

'Where are we going?' asked Amy, as he propelled her along a wide street. 'This is the way to the inn!'

'You surely heard Lord Father's orders,' said Crag. 'I must see you safe to the Maidens' Quarters.'

Amy jerked her arm away. 'What about my book?' she said stubbornly. 'You have to take me to the Bright One after sundown, and look—it's nearly that now. Come *on*, Crag!'

Crag sighed in exasperation.

'Amaryllis, you know I must play for the master at sundown. I shall return to the inn for you when I know my fate.'

'You promised!' cried Amy. She heard her voice growing high and out of control; other fairgoers paused to stare at them and the spellhound rumbled deep in his chest.

'Amaryllis! How dare you shame me so before the crowds!' cried Crag, angry and flushed. 'I shall come for you when I have performed and that is my word on it. Cease playing the spoilt babe and come to the inn.'

'Might I be of assistance?' enquired a voice, and there was the graceful Lord Random in his reinbeast cloak.

'No, I thank you,' said Crag curtly. 'My sister is in some slight distress and I am escorting her to the inn. Come, Amaryllis. We must go.'

He took her arm again and dragged her along the street to the inn where they had stayed last night. 'Inside, and go directly to the Maidens' Quarters,' he ordered. 'No, do not argue, Amaryllis! I shall return when I am done and send a message for you to meet me at the door.'

'Will the Overdame let me out again?' panted Amy.

'Curfew is not until well after sundown,' said Crag shortly. 'Until then!'

He left Amy at the door and sped off to the general quarters where he had presumably hidden his lute.

Amy waited. Sophie and Gillie had not returned, and so she was left to while away the time alone. She knew none of the other girls and the Overdame was poor company. She sat by the barred window and twiddled her plait between her fingers. She patted Red, and wondered whether Lord Michael had arranged for the hound's supper. She planned what she would write in the green book when she had it in her possession. She'd have to be careful: it wouldn't do to write herself somewhere else instead. She bit her lip, imagining the horror of finding herself in world after world and never the right one. But that was foolish, and she fell to mentally ticking off her preparations. It was like waiting for the boarding call of your plane . . .

She had on her new reinbeast mantle, with the charm given to her by the Bright One securely in its pouch. She was ready to leave at a moment's notice, as soon as the message should come.

The low sun was gilding the edges of the bars—then, suddenly, it wasn't. Amy looked up. The sun had wholly set. Where was Crag? Had he played for the master yet? Had he forgotten his promise? Had he won his apprenticeship and gone off with the master immediately, leaving her stranded? Or had he been turned away?

Amy bit the end of her plait. She'd miss being able to do that when she was back in her own body again.

She wondered what the time was.

She wondered what the date was.

Had the 13th come and gone?

She tried to remember how many days it had been since she had first woken in the round chamber. But perhaps the two times moved at different rates. Perhaps she'd make it home the same day she'd left. Or a year before. Or a hundred years later. Rip Van Amy. Perhaps she should specify the time and date in her writing.

Where was Crag?

It was becoming decidedly dark. She couldn't find the Bright One herself: she didn't know where she was staying. The Bright Pavilion could be anywhere. Unless . . . Amy sat up with a jerk.

The Bright Pavilion was probably one of the facets where the crimson reinbeast was on display. So she need not wait for Crag, she could go alone.

Hurriedly, she tightened her mantle.

Someone rapped on the door and the Overdame swept across the floor to answer the summons.

'Any messages for the maidens in my care must be left with me,' she said sourly.

'Dame, you know me well,' said an indignant voice and a young girl pushed her way into the room. 'I have a message for Miss Amaryllis Loveday,' she said. 'Is Miss Loveday here?'

Amy stepped forward. 'I'm here.'

The girl grinned. 'The message is from Crag Loveday, your brother. Sorry 'bout that, Miss!'

'That's all right,' said Amy. 'I was expecting one from him.' She stepped forward and Red moved up beside her like a shadow.

The girl nodded and, with a defiant look at the Overdame, Amy followed her down the stairs. 'He's waiting at the door for you,' said the girl. 'Get there yourself can you, Miss? I got work to do.'

'Thank you,' said Amy, and hurried on. She couldn't see Crag, but Lord Random was leaning against the door jamb. 'Have you seen Crag?' asked Amy, going up to him.

'I have,' said Lord Random. 'I have come from him in fact.'

Amy gaped at him.

'A message,' said Lord Random solemnly. 'Your brother's apologies, Miss Amaryllis, but he has been delayed. The master has many awaiting his attention.'

'How long will he be?' wailed Amy, and Red echoed her dismay with a snarl. Really, he did seem unsettled in Western Port—but how *could* Crag let her down like this?

Lord Random raised his brows. 'Who can say? But understand, Miss Amaryllis, this day is of great importance to your brother. Can you truly blame him if he puts his interests above your own? Of high matter though they may be?'

Amy seethed. She'd *kill* Crag for this betrayal. But now she must go to the Bright One on her own, and swiftly. She had wasted so much time sitting in the Maidens' Quarters like a good child, waiting for Crag to fulfil his promise.

'Thank you, Lord Random, for bringing me the message,' she said quickly. 'Now I've got to go.'

But Lord Random was shaking his head. 'Miss Amaryllis! Indeed you must do no such thing. Have you forgotten the woman who gave you pause this morning? I promise you, there are many of her stamp abroad this eve. Come, I shall escort you back to the Maidens' Quarters and give you into the care of the Overdame.'

'I am going *out*!' hissed Amy.

'Shall I go then to summon your lord father from his debates?'

'No!' She stamped her foot. 'Oh, you don't understand! I *must* go. Look, what's it to you, anyway?'

Lord Random's face went cold. 'You ask that of me, Amaryllis Loveday? I am not of the Nine Castles, but for all that you need not be so discourteous! I am, I hope, merely rendering some trifle of a service for someone who may one day be my benefactor. Come, I shall return you to the Overdame and all is mended.' He took her arm.

'No,' said Amy between her teeth. 'If you lay one more finger on me I'll—I'll scream, and say you're abducting me! Then Red will have you for dinner. See—he's growling already!'

Lord Random folded his arms and leaned back against the wall. 'You may do as you will,' he said in a cheerful tone, 'but you will not pass from the inn by this door. I would not have you fall in with . . . certain people.'

Amy felt tears welling. After coming so far and waiting so long, she couldn't bear to be baulked by this wretched man and his fusspot ways. OK, so he had saved her once—but probably the sewing dame wouldn't really have done any more than taunt her. 'Oh, why didn't Crag come?' she said. 'He *knew* I had to see the Bright One.'

Lord Random's face changed abruptly. 'You had appointment with the Bright One this eve, Miss Amaryllis?'

'At sundown!' said Amy bitterly. '*Now* do you see how late I am? Look—if you won't let me go myself, will you come with me? Quick—leave a message for my father if you must—we'll be back before him anyway.'

'A most determined lady,' murmured Lord Random.

Red gave another sudden snarl, and Amy looked down at him in surprise. His hackles were up.

Lord Random must have been surprised too, for he looked round sharply.

'Oh—that woman must be around somewhere!' said

Amy. She peered out the door. 'Isn't that her out there?'

'It well may be, so perhaps we had best leave your hound behind us,' said Lord Random, 'for we must move quickly and quietly, and the poor beast is obviously disturbed by her presence.'

'But what if she comes after me . . .?'

'Miss Amaryllis, I think I am the equal of any dark dame—even of that one,' said Lord Random.

'I'm supposed to keep Red with me.'

But Lord Random was adamant. 'Miss Amaryllis, I know that, but I do warn you, 'tis not wise to take a spellhound near those of the Seventh Castle.'

And perhaps he was right there, thought Amy, remembering the wistful look in Red's eyes when the Bright One had departed from Lord Michael's castle. What would happen to Red if she wrote herself home from the Bright Pavilion? Would the Bright One return him to Amaryllis, or would she keep him for herself? Perhaps after all . . .

'Oh all right!' she snapped. 'I'll leave him here. But come on!'

Lord Random beckoned a serving man. 'You! Take the animal in charge until a lady should come again to claim it.'

Red snarled again, and the man looked doubtful. 'Here—that there's a spellhound!'

'Do as you're bid!' snapped Lord Random, clapping his hands smartly enough to make Amy's ears ring. 'The animal will not harm you if you intend no harm.'

Amy frowned, not liking his manner. Lord Michael

was always polite, even to Sophie and Silent Thomas. Especially to Sophie and Silent Thomas. She hoped abruptly that this man was not betrothed to her double: he was obviously too big for his boots. But she really had no choice. She must see the Bright One, and if he would not let her leave the inn alone, then he would just have to go along with her. Since she wouldn't have Red, his protection might be handy.

'It's all right,' she said to the spellhound. 'Amaryllis will be back soon. Now don't you play up for this man.' But she heard an anguished howl as she followed Lord Random. She glanced behind, and saw jet-bead eyes glittering in the lamplight. The sewing dame nodded to her ironically. 'Miss Amaryllis Stargem has taken a new protector, I see!'

Lord Random drew himself up. 'Dame—it becomes you not to address a maiden of the Nine Castles in such a fashion. I know well the value Lord Michael places on the welfare of his kin, and so I tell you the part is played. You need not trouble Miss Loveday again.'

'So I see,' said the dame, and Amy shivered. What was it the woman had against her—or Amaryllis?

The streets were dark now, and Amy lifted her skirts high as she hurried along. To her relief, Lord Random seemed to have lost his desire for conversation: he offered his arm and after a moment Amy took it. There could be no harm: Crag and Lord Michael had done the same.

'I didn't think it was this far to the pavilion,' she panted at one point.

'Distances deceive after sundown,' said Lord Random. 'Your meeting with the Bright One must be vital indeed to bring you into the dark?'

Amy ignored this. 'We are supposed to be going to the Bright Pavilion,' she reminded. 'Surely that's in the Nine Castles Pavilion in the middle of the town?'

'The Bright One will not be at the pavilion,' said Lord Random. ''tis fully too long after sundown: she will have retired to her lodging. You would truly have ventured alone? Yet you need not fear: your birthchain protects you from such as may seek to curse you.'

Amy's doubts stirred. It didn't seem to have done too good a job with the sewing dame. 'I want to go to the pavilion,' she said firmly. 'That's where Crag said to go.'

'And so we may,' said Lord Random agreeably, 'if you are willing to risk curfew at the Bright One's actual lodgings.'

He had an answer for everything, so Amy gave up. Her doubts returned as they seemed to be leaving the town proper, but by then it was too late to do anything but hope he knew where he was going. They were heading towards the outer sweep of Western Port and there was nobody else in sight.

# 18. Amaryllis
## *Caz*

maryllis walked on down the street and she couldn't believe what she was doing. This strange world must have taught her courage, she thought, for never at home would she have ventured into the abode of a witch, not even with her birthchain and the spellhound for protection.

She knelt at the doorway and felt beneath the mat for the key the grandam had hidden.

'Hey, Amy!' A girl was leaning on the grandam's low fence, watching her. 'You been away?'

'Why do you ask?' Amaryllis drew back her hand.

'Haven't seen you around lately, that's all. I suppose— you know—Sharon and Caz?' The girl smiled uneasily. 'Didn't expect you here today, that's for sure.'

Amaryllis straightened up without the key.

'Don't blame you for lying low,' said the girl mysteriously. She stirred the ground with her toe. 'I did my turn last time. I got through OK, but geez, never again!

Katie nearly got copped in the Mart when she had her go. Scared the piss out of her.' The girl clapped a hand over her mouth. 'Only thing is, I don't know what to do with the stuff. Caz never said and I don't want it. I mean, I'd never be able to wear it anywhere. Mum always wants to know where I get stuff from and there's no way she'd ever believe the found-ten-bucks-in-the-street routine.'

Amaryllis stared. This girl seemed crazed.

'I brought it to Caz, but she's not here,' explained the girl. 'Must be at the mall already. D'you reckon I'd be breaking my oath if I stuck 'em in the letterbox?'

Amaryllis had no idea.

'Well, are you going down to the mall then?' said the girl.

'I am going nowhere,' said Amaryllis.

The girl behind the gate tilted her head and looked wary. 'You reckon? Well, in that case you'd better look out!' she said.

The blonde on the bicycle was weaving back up the street, followed by two others. 'Nearly zero hour, Day!' she said, ignoring the other girl. 'Caz had the funny feeling you mightn't show, so she sent us to help you along. You, too, Marina.'

'I know my way, I thank you,' said Amaryllis. 'I am visiting the gran.'

'Don't give me that,' said the blonde girl lazily. 'The old lady's down at the corner shop. You're on your own, Day, and today's the day. Come on! It's holiday fun time!'

'I shall wait for the gran,' said Amaryllis firmly. These

girls were alarming her now. She looked for the friendly one, the one called Marina, but she had fallen behind the others and wouldn't look at Amaryllis.

'You can see your granny later on if you don't get copped,' said the blonde girl briskly. 'Right now, you're coming with us.'

She opened the gate and put a friendly-seeming hand on Amaryllis' arm.

'Remove your hand. You are hurting me,' said Amaryllis distantly.

'So yell for the cops! Come on youse lot, let's get to the mall.'

'I tell you, I do not wish to go with you.'

The blonde sighed. 'Geez, why didn't you just stay home then?'

A dark girl took Amaryllis' other arm and between them they hustled her off down the road towards the busier part of the settlement, leaving the bikes jumbled against the fence.

'What if someone nicks 'em?' asked another of Amaryllis' captors, a sharp-faced person with ginger hair and eyebrows.

'Get someone to watch 'em,' advised the dark one. 'Here, Marina, you do it. Well go on! You're chicken anyway. We all know that.'

The friendly one gave Amaryllis an apologetic look and darted back. 'You tell Caz I'm looking after the bikes!' she yelled anxiously. 'You tell her you said to!'

'Yeah, yeah,' mocked the ginger girl.

'I do not wish to come,' said Amaryllis, pulling away.

'Oh, shut up, Day. You had it coming to you,' snarled the blonde.

'You will be sorry when the grandam returns,' warned Amaryllis. 'The girl you have left will tell her what you have done and she will come for you.'

'What, Marina!' hooted the ginger one. '*She'll* never say anything. She's afraid her tongue'll drop out if she talks. Takes this oath business reallll serious!'

Amaryllis was angry. It was clearly no use calling for help from passers-by. To anyone whose arm was not being held in a bruising grip, the four of them doubtless looked like a merry party of maids, walking down to the village market in search of bargains. Apart from the grandam, she knew no-one of authority to whom to appeal, no stewards or lawgivers, no people of the Nine Castles.

By now they had reached the marketplace, a wide paved area with trees sprouting weirdly from round earth patches amid the stone. Water poured, tinkling from a device of metal, and flowers bloomed in long low beds. No cars roared by: it was clearly a place for people travelling afoot.

Parties of boys and girls strolled up and down or sat at tables sipping brightly coloured drinks. A minstrel played a stringed instrument and passers-by hurled coins at his feet.

Goods were displayed on every side: some under roofs and within walls just like houses, others set out on wide tables as vast as that in the Great Chamber at home.

Two girls sat at one of the wooden tables, slowly consuming bags of cooked potatoes. Their fingers were greasy, but they seemed unworried. They looked up and one of them smiled.

'Hi, Amy! Long time no see!' she said in a light and friendly voice. Her face was delicate and her bones fine and slender. Clearly, a person of breeding. Amaryllis was much relieved.

'These girls,' said Amaryllis to the delicate one, 'have forced me here against my will.'

'Really?' The girl rounded her eyes. 'What did you do that for?' she asked the other three.

'You said we were to go get her, Caz!' The dark one sounded injured.

'I said to remind her to come, Barbie, that's all,' said the girl called Caz calmly. 'I thought she might have forgotten. You wouldn't do that to us though, would you, Amy?'

The ginger girl sniggered. 'She must've done. We caught her visiting her granny.'

'Are you sure?' asked Caz. 'I reckon she'd gone to the wrong house by mistake. You were really visiting me, weren't you, Amy? Only I'd already left.'

'I wished to see the gran,' said Amaryllis. 'I do not know you, so why would I visit? We are not kin.'

Caz looked puzzled. 'Not know me? Of course you know me! We're friends forever, all seven of us. Aren't we, Katie?'

'If you say so, Caz,' said the other girl at the table, stuffing food into her mouth.

'Maybe she's got amnesia,' said Caz thoughtfully. 'Is that what it is, Amy? Have you bumped your head or something? Is that why you haven't been about?'

'She's talking funny,' said Katie.

'Oh, Amy always talks funny,' laughed Caz. 'Sounds as if she's swallowed a dictionary sometimes. Hmm.'

She examined her fingernails, which were pointed and strangely lustrous. 'I'm glad you decided to come today, Amy. If the girls hadn't happened to meet you at your granny's place I'd have had to come around to remind you myself.'

'There would have been no need. I had no wish to come here,' said Amaryllis distantly.

'Oh, but *Amy!*' Caz smiled at her, and something momentarily unpleasant peered out from behind her eyes, 'It's your turn! You wouldn't want to miss it.'

'We've all done our bit,' said the blonde self-righteously. 'Even Marina. Katie got a really grouse haul, didn't you K?'

'Two CDs,' nodded the plump one proudly. 'Nearly got nicked, though.'

'Too bad she hasn't got a CD player, eh?' said the ginger girl with a smirk. 'Stick 'em in the microwave, Katie. See what happens.'

'No, it's Amy's turn today,' said Caz. 'What are you going to get for us, Amy?'

'A dictionary?' suggested the ginger one wittily.

'Yeah, a book!' chimed in the dark one. 'Make her nick a book!'

'I don't know,' said Caz. 'A book's not so easy. You can't just slip it into your pocket, and if you stick it up your jumper it makes a sort of square bulge . . . What do you say, Amy? Could you manage a book?'

'I have no coin,' said Amaryllis.

'You have no coin,' said Caz consideringly. 'Oh, I like that!' She laughed.

'Geez, you need more than a coin to buy a book, airhead,' said the dark girl.

'Who said anything about buying?' said the ginger one loudly. 'Geez, she's packing death, Caz. Worse than Marina!'

Caz shot her a tolerant look. 'Cool it, Barbie. You'll make her nervous and that's bad. For all of us.' She dropped her chip bag neatly into the nearest rubbish bin then wiped her fingers daintily on a square of fine paper. 'Come on, it's time,' she said. 'All set, Amy?' Her blue eyes held Amaryllis'.

Amaryllis stared back. It seemed that this girl's air of breeding was deceptive. This girl was trying to make her friend Amy into a thief. Well, *she* wasn't Amy.

'I shall never steal for such a one as you,' she said disdainfully.

'Aw, come on, Amy. It's not really stealing,' said the plump one. 'It's not like taking something from a *per*son. These shops have got so much stuff they never even miss it!'

'Anyway,' said the dark girl in a hard voice, 'they ask for it, don't they? Putting all that stuff out front and sticking the prices up so's we can't buy anything? Five dollars I get, would you believe? *A week*! Can't even go to the movies on that. Can't even get a video.'

'They expect people to take things,' said Katie persuasively. 'That's why they put the prices up so high, to make up for the stuff people nick. Isn't that right, Caz?'

'Yeah, so if you don't nick something now and then, you're just putting more money into *their* pockets,' said the ginger girl. 'You got to do it to get ahead. Like balance of trade.'

'So you see?' said Caz gently to Amaryllis. 'No need for all this talk about "stealing". It's just a bit of fun, really, just evening the odds. We'll cover for you.'

The others surged around Amaryllis, carrying her towards one of the open doorways, and the dark girl thrust her inside.

'Remember, Amy,' said Caz's warm and friendly voice. 'You're a part of this now, whatever you do.'

# 19. AMY
## *Tenth Castle*

A my stopped walking.

'Come, we must hasten,' said Lord Random persuasively, 'if wc are to reach the Bright One's lodgings before curfew.'

'Look,' said Amy, and she heard a faint quake in her voice. 'You're not trying to tell me she's staying way out here!'

'But where else?' asked Lord Random. He sounded amused. 'Would you expect a Mistress of Mystery to put up in a common inn?'

'Lord Father puts up in a common inn,' snapped Amy.

'Indeed.' Lord Random laughed. 'There are those who say Lord Michael Loveday is hop out o' kin—else why does he have such common taste?'

They had reached the edge of the cliff by now: it reared above them like some dark beast, a dragon almost, with a raggedly arched spine. A black entrance-way gaped like a mouth and Lord Random escorted her

168

inside. 'We must hasten,' he said again. 'There is light around the first turning.'

'The Bright One doesn't live *here*!' said Amy.

'No indeed,' said Lord Random out of the dark. 'But this is the way to her dwelling. 'tis well lit, I promise.'

Amy stumbled over a rock and around a corner and, as he had said, into a lit cavern.

Inside was a huge fireplace, seats and a table. It was quite crowded, but after one curious glance the occupants turned deliberately away.

Had she not known she was in a cave in the heart of a cliff, she would have thought this a room in a castle: perhaps another Great Chamber.

'You see,' said Lord Random. 'We of the Tenth Castle do live fully as well as you others of the Nine, lacking only the title and a fair share in the wealth. Come.'

'Where are we going?'

'The one we seek lodges beyond,' said Lord Random. 'Come, let me show you.' He led the way through the vast cavern, paused to remove a lantern from a niche in the wall, and passed into another passage. A smooth stone door barred the way and Lord Random raised his hand, his birthchain glinting in the fitful light of the lantern.

The door slid sideways with a sibilant whisper.

'How did you do that?' asked Amy nervously. She could see no electronic eye.

He laughed. 'A trifling charm of my companion's design, but effective! The birthchain bids the door. Thus wild beasts and such cannot open it.'

'What if you lose your chain?' asked Amy stolidly.

Lord Random laughed again. 'Never fear, Miss Amaryllis. Should that horror befall me, I know what the beasts do not. The door is keyed to words as well.'

Beyond that door the voices from the great cavern fell away, and the only sound was the faint pat of their feet on the stone. Another door appeared.

Amy was shivering now with cold and nervousness. She hated being so far inside the rock, and Lord Random was beginning to give her the creeps.

'Is this door the same?' she asked, to divert her mind, but Lord Random did not answer directly.

'Come but this little way more,' he said, 'and we shall embark.'

The passage ended abruptly in moonlit open air. There was plenty of noise now, for waves were tossing themselves on the smooth rock face, sending up a veil of drops. The spray stung and chilled, and Amy had to blink to focus her eyes. This was not the open ocean, but a strait, for several hundred metres away the meagre dark hump of an island rose abruptly out of the sea.

Lord Random bent and pulled on a rope. This brought a small boat nosing into the mouth of the cave.

Amy baulked. 'No . . .' she said, shivering and wrapping her mantle more closely around her shoulders.

'But yes, my lady!' said Lord Random. ''tis a short voyage and the only way to find the one we seek. Have no fear, the water shall not touch you.'

Bending suddenly, he scooped Amy up in his arms.

Just like a fairytale prince, thought Amy, but she was by no means enchanted. She was afraid—and furious.

'Put me down!' she said, but Lord Random only

laughed. Fear gave way abruptly to real terror: how could she have been so *stupid* as to leave the inn with Lord Random? Hadn't she been warned over and over about this sort of thing? Yet how could she not have come?

To have stayed at the inn would have been to miss her appointment with the Bright One and perhaps her only opportunity to get home.

Well, she was going to miss that appointment now in any case, she thought grimly, so she might just as well have stayed at the inn. I'll *kill* that Crag, she thought. If he'd come himself none of this would have happened!

'I'm not going in that boat,' she said aloud, and her voice shook.

'Indeed you are,' said Lord Random, still kindly. 'No need to fear.' He dumped her in the boat and held firmly to the collar of her mantle while he slipped the rope from around the projecting rock. He steadied the boat and jumped aboard.

There was no need to push the craft off: it slewed immediately into the current.

'Ah,' said Lord Random with satisfaction as the boat crested a wave. 'I feared we would miss the tide! Now 'tis almost on the turn and no boatman can hope to pit his strength against the waves, even if he knows the sea. This, Amaryllis, is the Gullet: many an unwary one has been swallowed by it!'

Amy sat up. The cave mouth was receding: Lord Random had left the lantern on a rock. She thought about jumping into the water, but dismissed the idea immediately. He would catch her before she had swum three strokes.

'What, naught to say, Amaryllis?' he was asking. No 'Miss' or 'my lady' from him now.

'You're a creep,' said Amy.

Lord Random laughed and dropped the rest of his pretence. 'The Cold Isle is not without shelter,' he said. 'We have prepared a special chamber for your stay. It will not be a long one, if Michael is sensible.'

Amy scowled. This was a kidnapping and she had walked right into it. She had come willingly with Lord Random and there were plenty back at the inn to swear so. No doubt a ransom demand would be sent to Lord Michael and it was all her fault. And Crag's.

She could have wept with the irony of it: Lord Michael would end up paying a ransom for a girl who was not even his daughter. If she were brave enough, she should tell Lord Random just that—that he had kidnapped the wrong girl. But the truth sounded so improbable—why should he believe her?

The current swept the boat around behind the island, and Lord Random backwatered with the oars and called out. From the shore a lantern light sprang out: obviously a signal.

The boat rode in on the waves and a cloaked figure put down the light and caught the rope which Lord Random tossed ashore.

'A success, as you may see!' he said. The other person's face and form were in shadow, but a pair of finely made shoes stepped forward into the light while the rope was made fast.

'Now, we must hurry and settle our guest in her quarters,' said Lord Random. A sharp tug brought Amy to her feet, and she climbed unsteadily—and most unwillingly—out of the boat and stood trembling on the bare rock landing stage.

'Come,' said Lord Random, and the cloaked one picked up the lantern, turned, and led the way around the rocks and into the entrance of another cave.

Amy dragged her heels as much as she could, but she knew it was useless. Obviously there was no-one on this windswept place to rescue her, and even if she ran now she wouldn't get far in the rock-strewn dark.

They passed through another twisted passage: was it natural or had it been chipped out of the rock? Suddenly, the light was thrown upon what appeared to be a dead end, Lord Random stepped forward and the rock slid sideways. He pushed Amy ahead into a small room containing a chair, an unlit lantern, a jug of water and nothing else.

'You'd be uncomfortable here, I fear, should your stay be a long one,' said Lord Random, bowing.

'You can't keep me here,' said Amy. 'There's no point. I'm not Amaryllis Loveday.'

Lord Random stared, then smiled at her kindly. He reached out and touched the chain around her neck. 'Of course you are, my dear,' he said, still kindly. 'Do you not wear the stargem birthchain of the Fifth Castle? Do you not wear reinbeast weave of the finest quality, symbol of the Fourth? And were you not accompanied by the spellhound of the Seventh? A rich double prize you are, to be sure. Ah, Amaryllis, had you but kept the spellhound at your side I could hardly have fetched you away so easily.'

'But the sewing dame—you saved me from the sewing dame!' blurted Amy.

Lord Random laughed. 'Oh, and what a merry charade that was indeed! My lady mother played her part to a nicety, did she not? And so coaxed you to accept my escort! Ah yes, Amaryllis, Lady Cazani of the Tenth is skilled in her way—she learned much from your so-liberal lord father, and much from the cook maid before her dismissal: neatly staged, was it not? And yet it gave her the measure of the hound. Be sure she will by now have subdued the beast in such a way he'll never again lift the lip at his betters.'

'Don't you hurt Red!' croaked Amy.

Lord Random was still holding the birthchain, twisting it between his fingers, making the stargems wink in the light. 'Hurt him? No more than draw his teeth lest we anger my lady here—but for yourself you need have no fear,' he said gently. 'Your birthchain will ward off harm, will it not?'

Amy nodded, then wished she had not as the chain tightened. 'So you might as well take me straight back now,' she said. 'And let Red go.'

'But how if you are *not* wearing the birthchain?' suggested Lord Random.

Nice try, punk, thought Amy. It won't come off.

'My lady! Of your courtesy light the other lamp,' said Lord Random. The cloaked one with the lantern did so, then stepped forward. With bewilderment Amy recognised the butterfly robes of the Bright One.

174

Had Lord Random kept part of his word after all? Amy began to speak, falling over her words to explain why she had been delayed, and asking for the return of her book. 'I know Sophie gave it to you,' she said, 'but that was a mistake . . . and you'll not let Red be hurt, he loves you so much . . .'

The Bright One glanced at her indifferently. 'This is the maid for sure?' she asked Lord Random.

'It is,' he said. 'The lad would perhaps have been the better choice, but this prize was so easily won!'

The Bright One's eyes were contemptuous as she reached out and took hold of the birthchain. A quick twist of her hands and the fine links came apart.

Released, Amy staggered backwards and fell.

The Bright One dropped the broken chain in Lord Random's hand and swept out.

'Wait!' cried Amy desperately, but the door had closed.

Lord Random shook his head. 'You see, Amaryllis,' he said sympathetically. 'You *will* be staying here after all, with neither hound nor birthchain to warn nor ward. You have been rather foolish, have you not?'

Amy shivered. 'Wh-when will you let me go?' she asked.

'As to that,' said Lord Random over his shoulder. 'Michael will get the birthchain on the morrow—and perhaps some small token from the hound. He shall then have some days—is not that generous?—to deliver a pair of prime reinbeast and a casket of stargems to a certain place. In return he will have news of his daughter. But perhaps that is not a good bargain . . . word has it he favours his daughter above most things and he has recently enjoyed a singular and most undeserved piece of fortune . . . What if we require the golden reinbeast as well? He has had it so little time he'll not miss it."

Lord Random lifted his hand and the door opened. 'By the way,' he added mockingly. 'I'd not try to open this door were I you. The Lady Amaryllis Loveday will never pass this threshold without her birthchain. My bright lady assures me of that.'

Amy stared at him numbly. What if he took away the lamp and left her in the dark, alone? She couldn't take that!

'Besides,' Lord Random added gently, 'there is really no point in leaving this chamber, even could you summon the words to do so. My lady and I shall sail immediately with the tide, and I assure you there is no other vessel on this rock. Rest well, Amaryllis Loveday. You'll not see me again—should your lord father co-operate.'

The door slid closed behind him.

## 20. Amaryllis

# Wrong

'I am part of nothing concerning you,' said Amaryllis disdainfully to herself, but she was within the building now and the way out was barred by the girls who had followed her.

'Are you looking for anything in particular, dear?' asked the stallholder. She wore round spectacles through which she peered at Amaryllis.

'I was admiring your wares,' said Amaryllis quickly.

If she were to approach this friendly person and tell her how she was being forced to be a thief, what then would the girls do? Run, for certain. But—would they come back on another occasion and practise their wickedness then? For it was wickedness, for all the girl Caz tried to make game of it. Had Red been here, thought Amaryllis, he would have howled a warning long ago.

Red was far away and she knew she might never see him again, but still she could feel the wrong here for

177

herself. Perhaps anyone could develop spellhound power should they but choose.

And if she stole a ledger from this harmless stallholder through fear, she would feel the wrong for the rest of her days and Red would sense it in her and hate her presence.

One of the other girls stepped forward and cleared her throat, deliberately removing the stallholder's attention from Amaryllis.

'Can I help you?' the stallholder asked again.

'Yeah, well . . .' The girl giggled. It was Barbara, the dark one. 'There's this book, see . . .' She giggled again and nudged the ginger girl, who rolled her eyes.

'Shut up, you dork!' said the ginger girl.

'Which book is this?' asked the woman. 'Do you know the title?'

Barbara looked blank. 'I don't know. Can't remember. Can you, Kylie?'

'Who wrote it then?'

The ginger girl shrugged. 'Don't ask me! Wendy's always doing this to me!'

Wendy? The girl's name was Barbara—wasn't it? Then Amaryllis saw their game. These two were keeping the stallholder's attention away from what Amaryllis was doing. It was wasted effort, since Amaryllis was doing nothing.

There had to be a way out of this.

The two at the counter didn't look her way once, but simply went on with their inane posturing. There were two others in the shop, however, and the blonde girl called Sharon was watching Amaryllis and jerking her head to indicate the shelves at the rear of the stall.

Amaryllis ignored the summons. What if she created a diversion of her own?

What if she started a scuffle with fat Katie and knocked over some of the wares? Would not the stall-holder send them away in anger?

But then these girls would come back with another puppet and do their work.

Outside on the sunny paving, sitting at her table, the girl Caz sipped a drink and gazed at the sauntering crowds. She was the sly one, for she planned and com-pelled in the shadows. One who set herself up against this Caz would pay. If others could be made to share the load . . .

Amaryllis wandered over to where Katie was examin-ing small coloured pictures on a stand.

Katie's hands were shaking.

Excellent.

'If we are found stealing in this place,' murmured Amaryllis, 'you and I shall be punished.'

Plump Katie put down the coloured pictures and edged away.

'These others also—they will perhaps be punished,' continued Amaryllis.

'Shut up and get *on* with it!' begged Katie.

'Caz, who sits beneath the sky and looks the other way, she will not be punished,' said Amaryllis.

'No—well, we took an oath not to split,' said Katie. 'You know that.'

'I took no oath,' said Amaryllis.

Sharon was glaring at Amaryllis by now and her signals were sharp and pre-emptory.

Perhaps she could simply turn about and walk out? Would they follow?

'Yeah, well, it's this really good book my cousin said, all about this girl,' said Barbara, 'and she joins this club, and she's doing really well and then suddenly her mum says she's getting a divorce and the girl . . .'

Amaryllis edged around behind a stand of goods. If she could slip out while the others were busy perhaps she could get away.

'Oh dear,' said the stallholder sympathetically. 'That could be any one of a dozen or more books. It would help if you could remember the title, or even the character's name!'

The ginger girl sniggered.

Sharon stepped around the stand of goods and took hold of Amaryllis' arm. 'Get on with it, Day,' she said. 'Or else.'

Amaryllis glanced around. Sharon, Katie and the ginger girl were looking at her menacingly.

Perhaps she should call aloud to the stallholder, but would the woman take her word against so many?

Twisting against Sharon's painful grip, Amaryllis put out her hand and obediently chose the richest, largest volume she could find and slipped it from the shelf.

# 21. CRAG

# *Master*

There were many more hopeful apprentices in Western Port than Crag had expected, and the standard of those he heard playing was frighteningly high. It was some while after sundown when his turn finally came, and he was nervous, and felt he played poorly.

The master, however, smiled kindly and asked him to join the handful of lads and men who had been chosen to play again. So he still had a chance!

Crag drew a shaky breath and fondled his lute. When his next turn came he would play with more assurance. He would play so well that the master would decide in his favour. He knew he could do it.

But several still awaited their first performance, and it came to him that at this rate he could not hope to return to the inn in time to escort his sister on her quest.

Did it matter? he wondered. The quest was, at best,

that of a child deprived of a favoured possession: a ledger!

Would he not buy her a dozen when he was made master? A lost ledger could not compare in importance to a man's whole future.

But perhaps it was not truly the ledger she sought, but some token from the Bright One. Amaryllis was always eager for charms and omens. If so, it was still not of great import: there would be another day.

Yet he disliked letting her down. He had given his word and he would like to keep it, somehow. It came to him that he could explain the matter to Lord Michael if he saw him on the morrow, and his father—no matter how angered with Crag—would see to it that Amaryllis was not disappointed. If he could just send word to her now and reassure her of this, then his conscience could be wholly quieted and he could give of his best for Master Ash.

As he sat fretting among the other fortunate ones, he was suddenly hailed from the outer circle. Turning, he was not altogether pleased to see Lord Random; the man was affable enough but he had an unruly tongue. Lord Random, though, was delighted to see Crag and said complimentary things about his performance. He was only sorry, he said, that he could not stay for the final rounds and the selection. 'For music of this calibre is seldom heard where I dwell,' he said. 'We who are not of the Nine Castles must make shift with what we have.'

Crag mumbled something. This was the tune Lord Random played perpetually.

'I am puzzled, though,' continued Lord Random.

'Were you not to escort Miss Amaryllis somewhere this eve? Yet I do not see her in this company.'

Crag nodded. 'I am delayed and I fear she will not be pleased,' he said shortly. 'If I could but send a message to assure her . . .'

Lord Random bowed. 'Then I shall be your courier!' he said. 'For the Western Inn lies in my own direction.'

Crag thought quickly. He didn't particularly like the man, but the offer seemed sincere. 'Then tell her I shall be late,' he said. 'Say she is not to fear, her commission will surely be carried out.'

Lord Random repeated the message word for word, bowed gracefully and went on his way. Crag shook his head, suddenly remembering the Overdame at the inn. He had been unable to pass her last eve, and he was brother to one of her charges!

Yet surely one such as Lord Random would find a way to slip past her guard and, besides, the man was gone now.

Another hopeful minstrel began to play, stumbling over the opening chords. Crag promptly put the matter of Amaryllis from his mind, satisfied that he had acted honourably. To be sure, his lord father might not be pleased with his choice of courier, but that was all of a piece, and doubtless he would have been less pleased had Crag sent none at all.

Much later, Crag bowed to the master and left the pavilion in a state of shock.

He'd thought himself prepared for rejection. He'd vowed that, should it come, he would put away all thought of minstrelsy and learn an interest in matters of the Fourth Castle. It was simple, he had thought. He would play for Master Ash, the master would say one thing or the other: 'Come then and be my apprentice' or 'Return to your lord father'.

He had never thought the master would lay forms and conditions, ask questions and speak of sense and duty.

And what was he now to do? Go to Lord Michael and beg his indulgence?

Crag bit his lip. In any case he must go to the inn and face whatever might come in the morning. He glanced at the sky: it was much too late to send word to Amaryllis now.

He reached the inn, but before he could enter he was waylaid by a cry from the doorway. 'Oh, Master Crag, you are back at last!'

Crag sighed. The last thing he needed now was trouble with his mother's tower maid. But one must be polite. 'Well, Sophie, have you a problem?' he asked. He saw Sophie's betrothed hovering at her shoulder and nodded pleasantly to the man.

'Oh, Master Crag!' cried Sophie, with obvious relief. 'I have been so worried: Lady Jasmin put Miss Amaryllis in my care—the Overdame says she was here and left again with you!'

Crag stared. 'Not at all, Sophie. I but sent her a message. She is still safe in the Maidens' Quarters.'

'The Overdame says not, master. Your message was delivered and Miss left the quarters to go to you. Oh, Master Crag, had I been here I would have prevented it!'

'I'm sure you would,' said Crag. His spirits sank. The little *fool*. She had been angered by his message and had gone to the Bright One alone.

'I shall go after her,' he said quickly. 'No fear, Sophie, she will be safe enough and I shall have her back here betimes.' He hoped.

But Sophie's tears showed no sign of abating and even merry-faced Jarman looked concerned.

'She has but gone to the Bright One!' said Crag testily.

'She cannot have done so! She has left the spellhound behind her!'

'She never would,' said Crag definitely. 'I had not thought she would venture out unescorted, but to leave the hound! Never!'

Sophie nodded tearfully. 'The hound is here, and I fear great harm is about, for a dame unknown came to take it hence. The hound would by no means go; a tapster intervened and the dame cursed Lord Michael and left in no good order.'

'Then I must go to the Bright Pavilion,' said Crag. 'No, Sophie, you stay. Should she return, take her to the Maidens' Quarters. Should my lord father return—have Thomas tell him all.'

## 22. CRAIG
# *Team*

raig didn't enjoy the water polo trials as much as he had expected. It was noisy and rowdy, and he certainly acquitted himself well enough, but somehow his sister's face kept coming between him and the ball.

Blast her, he thought angrily.

His foot slipped and he hit the water face first, stinging his eyes and hurting the back of his nose. It felt like a rush of tears in reverse, and Craig spluttered and groped his way to the side of the pool to recover.

And of course that reminded him of Amy again.

Had she really gone schizzo? If so, he ought to have told Mum and Dad long ago. If she was just playing some game with him, well then, let her get into trouble. It wasn't *his* fault if she acted the goat once too often. But he didn't think she was playing a game. Why should she? And why keep it up for so long?

Sometimes she was so convincing that he almost

caught himself believing her preposterous story.

That was bad enough, but it was even worse to suspect that she believed it herself.

'Hey, Craig! Get yourself over here!' yelled Jason. With relief, Craig dived again for the ball. He wasn't used to thinking about his sister.

He made his place on the team, but it wasn't the thrill he expected.

'Coming for a pizza?' asked Jason afterwards.

Craig was overcome with after-swimming starvation but he shook his head regretfully. 'Nah, said I'd pick Amy up at Gran's. She's not real well.'

'Yeah?' said Jason. 'What's up with her?'

Craig shrugged. 'Dunno. Guts-ache, probably. Girls get 'em sometimes.' He draped his towel around his neck and rode away.

He was sure Amy didn't have a guts-ache, but there was no way he'd admit to a schizzo sister, not to motor-mouth Jason.

He pedalled to Gran's place in his best racing style. He hoped Amy hadn't been shooting her mouth off—but perhaps it would be just as well if she had. If she came the Amaryllis stunt on Gran, then Gran would be the one responsible for putting her in to Jan and Mike. In any case, Gran ought to be good for a milkshake and probably a bit of banana cake as well. Gran's banana cake was famous: almost worth missing out on the pizza.

He parked his bike by the fence.

A skinny kid was sitting on the dusty grass verge with her chin on her knees. Craig flicked her a glance. Not

Amy, and not the Brandon girl, but about their age.

He opened Gran's door and stuck his head in. 'Ammo? Gran? You there?'

'That you, Craig?' yelled Gran's voice.

'Yeah—come to pick up Amy,' said Craig, letting himself into the house. 'Got a bit of cake in the pantry?'

'Well there's a funny thing!' said Gran, trundling out of the kitchen.

'Yeah? Amy's ate it all?'

'No, Amy herself. She *was* here,' said Gran. 'Met her down the road when I was going to the corner shop. She said she'd go ahead and put the jug on, but when I got here she hadn't done it. Key still under the mat and all.'

'Probably over at Caz Brandon's,' said Craig uneasily.

'I thought she'd fallen out with that Caz?'

Craig grunted. 'Might've fallen in again.'

'Oh well—she'll be back,' said Gran. 'Come and have a cuppa.'

But Craig shook his head. 'Best go and find her,' he said. 'See ya!'

He went out to get his bike and this time he stopped near the skinny girl in the gutter. 'You're a friend of Amy's, aren't you?' he said.

The girl squinted up at him. 'Yes.'

'Seen her round lately?

The girl looked away.

'Look, I know she was here about an hour ago,' said Craig. 'She gone in there?' He pointed to the Brandon house.

'No,' she said.

'You have seen her then?' Craig felt a bit silly, giving

the kid the third degree. He was tempted to go straight home, but if Amy wasn't there he'd be back to square one. 'Look,' he said uneasily. 'I'm her brother, right? I got to take her home. She's crook.'

The girl raised alarmed eyes. 'They went down to the mall,' she said.

'Who's they?'

She shook her head, and Craig gave up in exasperation. 'Thanks a bundle, spazzbrain,' he said unkindly, and wheeled his bike out onto the road.

Behind him, the skinny kid began to cry.

# 23. AMY
## The Gullet

he chamber seemed very empty after Lord Random had gone. The floor was chill, so Amy scrambled to her feet and drew her mantle around her. It was cold. But then it would be, she thought, in the middle of a cliff in the middle of an island in the middle of the sea. She gave a kind of hysterical giggle at the thought, which quickly became a sob, but there was no point in crying. There was no-one to hear and no-one to help. All the same, she did cry, as much for poor betrayed Red as for herself. He had so worshipped that Jadetha, and now look!

When she had finished, she scooped up a handful of achingly cold water from the jug and splashed it over her face. Some went down her collar and she shivered. How, she wondered drearily, was she going to get out of this one?

Like the situation at home with Caz, she could see

clearly enough how she had got into it—but, again, she couldn't see any way out.

She was stuck here until Lord Michael ransomed her with reinbeast.

That was more of a sacrifice than it sounded. Possession of a pair of reinbeast would mean that Lord Random would be able to set himself up as Lord Michael's equal. Well, all people were equal, but why should a creep like Lord Random use her to benefit from years of somebody else's hard work?

Kidnappers—particularly the sort that pretended to be helping you—were the pits.

And, meanwhile, Amy had missed her appointment with the Bright One. Not that that mattered now, since the Bright One had proved herself as bad as Lord Random.

Lord Michael's words floated back: 'I fear the Bright One will one day request a pair of prime reinbeast and that I shall be tranced into giving her her will.'

Well Jadetha hadn't done that. She had gone into partnership with Lord Random and his sewing-dame mother instead.

Ugh. Amy kicked the leg of the chair. The Bright One was a creep. A creepess. All that about meeting her at sundown had been a trick from the start. She could just as well have given Crag the book when he asked for it.

Was Crag mixed up in this? He *had* set up the meeting with the Bright One. He *had* sent Lord Random to the inn.

Or had he?

She had no actual proof that Lord Random had come

from Crag. He might have made up the message himself. She should have demanded to see Crag's note. Except that she wouldn't have recognised his handwriting anyway. Though Lord Random would not have realised that.

Amy's head ached and whirled, and the more she tried to work things out, the worse it all seemed to become. None of it really made sense. Lord Random must know he couldn't get away with this: Lord Michael wouldn't allow it. Oh, he'd probably hand over the reinbeast pair but then, once he had Amy back, he'd sool the law on to Lord Random for sure. You couldn't just go around kidnapping people's daughters and hurting spellhounds and then expect to be left in peace to breed your ill-gotten reinbeast!

That was when she had the nastiest thought of all. Lord Michael would never know for sure who had kidnapped her—unless she told him. It followed that Lord Random, his mother and the Bright One would make jolly sure she never did tell him, and *that* meant they wouldn't be letting Amy go.

Ever.

Which meant that Lord Michael would have sacrificed the reinbeast and his status in the Nine Castles for nothing.

'Well, sorry about that, Lord M,' muttered Amy, 'but what about me? I'll be sacrificed too and I'm not even the one they wanted!'

She whipped up her anger. It was the only way to keep from sliding into despair.

She didn't know how long she sat there waiting.

Nothing happened and nobody came, and soon even her anger couldn't keep her warm. She slid her hand into the pouch of her mantle. No CB radio or magic keys or even a file. Not that a file would be much good against that stone door.

Her fingers closed on the coin given to her by the Bright One at the castle.

Spying out the land, just like that sewing dame, thought Amy savagely. Sucking up to Lady J. Giving me presents!

She flipped the luckpiece into the air and it fell with a muffled *tunking* sound. It had rung like silver at the castle. Amy picked it up and saw it was now dull and grey: not shining any more.

'Huh!' she said and stuck it back in her pouch. It was obviously worthless, but still she wasn't leaving it here for the Bright One's next victim.

Bright One indeed! Creepy One more likely. That woman really could act. Look how she'd come over all gracious in front of Lady J! And how she'd conned poor Red with her smiling eyes! She'd been like another person.

Having nothing else to do, Amy worried around that notion until she tracked it down to its source. The eyes. The Bright One at the castle had had odd coloured eyes. One blue and one green.

The Bright One who had broken her birthchain—the creepess—had had odd eyes as well. Iron-grey and indifferent. But both the same.

*Had* it been a different woman then? She certainly

hadn't seemed to recognise Amy . . .

'A luckpiece, child of the castle, child of the crag. Remember the Bright One, and surely the Bright One will remember you.'

That lilting voice was quite different from the cold tones she had heard in this room.

Had there been *two* Bright Ones? Twins? That might be the explanation, and if so it was very interesting, but it didn't get her out of this mess.

Amy glared malevolently at the door. She couldn't see a lock, but Lord Random had warned her plainly.

Lady Amaryllis Loveday would not be able to walk through that door without her birthchain.

She'd always thought that birthchain thing was a lot of superstitious rubbish, like wearing a lucky tiki or not breaking mirrors, but now it began to look as if it had something in it, like the sewing dame's enchanted pin. Certainly Lord Random must believe in the birthchain if he were willing to leave her in here with the door unlocked just because he had taken the thing away.

She wondered what would happen if she *did* try to get out. Zings of lightning? Electric shocks? Poisoned darts? Or wouldn't they bother? After all, this door was only the first barrier.

Sleeping gas?

She didn't fancy that, but neither did she fancy hanging about to be used as a lever by Lord Random. And possibly left to die here by Lord Random at the end of it all.

Perhaps there was another way out?

She prowled around the chamber, but the walls were

solid stone. No good rapping on *that* for hollow spots, but she tried anyway and bruised her knuckles. The floor and ceiling were natural rock too. At least, she thought with a shudder, there were no bats. They were animals: they couldn't get in.

She glanced up to where the lantern hung. What if it went out? She'd be alone in the dark and nobody but Lord Random and the creepess and probably the sewing dame would know she was there.

To keep herself from panic, Amy prowled again. Her eyes were drawn once more to the stone door. It was smooth and bluish, like slate.

Daringly, she reached out and brushed the door with the back of her hand.

No lightning. No hiss of poison gas.

Had Lord Random been bluffing?

Lady Amaryllis Loveday will never walk through that door without her birthchain.

She knew something Lord Random did *not* know. She was not Amaryllis Loveday. No doubt Amaryllis would be horrified at the loss of her birthchain. Amy knew better. She hoped.

She *wasn't* Amaryllis. That was her only advantage and she was going to play it for all she was worth.

Drawing the mantle more tightly around her, Amy laid both palms flat against the door. She pressed it sideways. For a moment she thought it moved, but it was only her hands, slipping on the stone. Her palms stung.

It was so cold that her breath formed a vapour as she rubbed her hands together.

She wished she'd taken more notice on the way in. How had horrible Lord Random opened it?

By simply raising his hand. With the birthchain.

Well, she had no birthchain, but she could certainly raise her hand. And she'd push up and down and from side to side . . .

The door opened.

It was pitch dark outside.

'Wow-iss-imo!' breathed Amy. She had never expected it to work.

But now it had—she took down the lantern, and held it high. There was the stone passage, just as before. The lack of her birthchain had made no difference at all, once she had put her mind to it, but whether this was because Lord Random had been bluffing or because she was not Amaryllis Loveday, she had no way of telling.

She couldn't hang round here. If Lord Random came back and caught her, he'd make sure she didn't get out again. There'd be no more binding with bluff. Next time he'd use rope and take away the light. She couldn't bear that.

Amy found that she was sweating, despite the dank chill, and put down the lantern to wipe her palms on her skirt. Then she started off along the tunnel.

It seemed long and uneven, and she didn't dare stumble for fear of dropping the lantern. Without light she would be helpless.

So she placed her feet like a tightrope walker: carefully.

The path was cold and hard and nerve-racking, but Amy could have wished it would never end. The next bit would be worse, much worse, and there was an excellent chance that she would not survive what she intended to do. But she was going to do it: no doubt about that. And she was going to do it precisely because Lord Random was so certain she wouldn't dare.

She rounded a bend in the tunnel and a surge of fresh salt air met her face. And it was actually daylight. Well, dawn, anyway.

It was also warmer in the open air than it had been in the depths of the caves, though not by much. Amy cringed back into the doorway. What if Lord Random were spying on the mouth of the cave? But he wasn't: he couldn't be unless he had the Hubble Telescope in his pocket. As far as she could see there was ocean— cold, grey and foam flecked. Of course, she was on the wrong side of the rocky island.

She blew out the lantern and climbed carefully around until she was nearly opposite the narrow strait. She stumbled over a rock and slopped some of the lantern fuel: it didn't smell like petrol or kerosene. Perhaps it was some sort of oil?

Well, oil had more uses than fixing squeaky doors and frying fish! She continued more cautiously.

The flat rock where the boat had been was slick with salt water, and Amy stood and shivered as she waited for her eyes to become accustomed to the early light. Then she stared at the waves until she was sure the tide was still running around towards the cliffs. Even by peering as hard as she could, she could make out no details in the cliffs opposite: perhaps the cave mouth was too far around to be seen from here.

She leaned against the rock and winced as the damp soaked through her skirts. Full daylight would bring more danger. There was nothing more to gain by waiting: nothing but more fear. So she slowly unhooked the thick stockings from the legs of her drawers. She untied the petticoat from her waist and then, with a shudder, took off her mantle and dress. The dress, stockings and petticoat she rolled up and wedged into a cleft in the rock, then she wadded up the mantle and twisted it into a knot. The sleeves formed a loop.

The lantern oil felt and smelt disgusting, but Channel swimmers always used it so who was she to turn up her nose? Amy slathered handfuls of the stuff over her arms and legs and coated as much of her body as she could under the shift. She slid the looped sleeves of the mantle over her head and one shoulder, settling the bulk of it around the back where it made a warm patch. Then she stepped out onto the flat rock.

As she stood there shaking with cold and terror, she knew that she hadn't really meant to do it. She'd been sure Lord Random would pop out from behind a rock and hustle her back to captivity.

The water was cold, and stingingly salty.

'Don't forget—the sea isn't the local pool,' warned Jan's voice in her mind. 'No matter how good a swimmer you think you are, you must not go into the water alone.'

If I ever get out of this, thought Amy, I won't. The water surged suddenly from knee deep to the middle of her thighs, and a wave lifted her off her feet. She gasped as the cold gulped her down, terrified of being dashed against the rock. But the tide was flowing away round the island and should carry her with it towards the cliffs. If she didn't freeze first.

The current swept outwards and around, and Amy was too breathless to do anything but go with the tide. The water was just as salty as the sea at home, and she could make out unpleasant eddies that were probably whirlpools.

By now she couldn't have got back to the island if she had tried, but she trod water and tried to see which way she was headed. The waves heaved and receded and sometimes she could see nothing but the dull green water. Then she'd rise to the top and see the darker grey of land. If only it wasn't so cold! She rolled onto her side and began to swim with a cautious sidestroke. Speed wasn't important here. Stability was. One mouthful of water and the crouching panic would pounce.

Amy was soon exhausted; despite the help of the tide it was immensely difficult to keep her head above water. She couldn't understand it; she'd swum in colder water than this and for much longer. But now her arms and legs seemed lined with lead and her lungs refused to do their work. Her long hair washed loose from its braid and swirled around her shoulders, binding and hindering.

Her hair? Amaryllis' hair!

And that was surely the core of what was happening to her. In spirit, she was Amy Day, champion under-fourteen swimmer at the last regatta.

In body, she was Amaryllis Loveday, who had probably never swum in her life.

The inner Amy knew what to do and directed the body

to do it; the outer Amaryllis sagged and faded with exhaustion.

Float then, thought Amy. Turn on your back and float. Keep your face up; you won't breathe in the water. Move your hands and feet. *Do* it!

But as she rolled over and began to kick, she saw with horror that rather than simply washing back towards the cliffs, the water ahead was twisting and swirling in a cauldron of foam.

Amy abruptly forgot her plan of letting the waves carry her to shore and struck out for her life, but the racing water sucked her down with a burp of satisfaction.

She screamed, and a gush of bubbles rose from her mouth. Beyond the terror was absolute disbelief: that she, Amy Day, first cousin to a dolphin, could possibly be drowning in a narrow stretch of water in a world that was not her own.

And, oh God! If she drowned her borrowed body, what would happen then?

# 24. AMARYLLIS
## *Bottle*

hat're you doing?' hissed Sharon, pinching Amaryllis' arm painfully. 'You'll get copped if you take that!'

Amaryllis jerked away from her and approached the counter.

The stallholder looked down at her.

'Found something you want, dear?'

'This one,' said Amaryllis as firmly as she could. Now Barbara, Katie and the foxy ginger girl were staring at her in horror.

The stallholder reached out for the book. Even in that moment Amaryllis found time to notice that she handled it as if she loved it. 'This is a beauty, isn't it?' she said, pulling out a long sheet of brownish paper and beginning to wrap the book. 'Is it a present?'

Amaryllis shook her head.

'For you?' The stallholder's eyebrows climbed beyond the upper rims of her spectacles. Behind Amaryllis,

201

the other four girls began to sidle towards the door.

'I'll be with you in a minute, girls,' said the stallholder pleasantly. She turned back to Amaryllis.

'That'll be forty-nine dollars and ninety-five cents, dear.'

Amaryllis bit her lip.

'Oh dear,' said the woman. 'Haven't you got enough money? Well I'll tell you what we'll do—how about we make it a layby?'

'What is that?' asked Amaryllis.

'You can give me the money you have with you today,' said the woman, 'and then when you get more you can come in and pay it off. Meanwhile, I'll keep your book safe for you. You won't have to worry about it being sold to someone else. Is that what you'd like to do, Amy? It *is* Amy, isn't it? I thought I'd seen you in here before.'

'That is very generous,' said Amaryllis, 'but it will not be necessary. The book is not for me but for the one who sits in the sun.' She pointed through the doorway.

The woman looked puzzled. 'I'm not sure I know what you mean, dear?'

'It is simple,' said Amaryllis. 'The girl Caz . . .'

'Shut *up*!' hissed Sharon from the side. Her hand shot out to grab Amaryllis.

'No, let her finish,' said the stallholder, a pucker of frown between her eyes. 'And you wait there.'

'The girl Caz told me to get her a ledger—a book,' went on Amaryllis. 'I told her I had not the coin, but she said no matter. I was to get it.'

The woman gave a funny little half-smile and shook

her head. 'Curiouser and curiouser!' she commented. 'We'll have to get to the bottom of this. You—' she pointed to Katie. 'Do you know the girl out there?'

Katie's eyes bulged, but she nodded slightly.

'Good. Then will you ask her to come in?'

Katie shook her head in panic.

The woman sighed. 'Wait here.' She strode across to the doorway and put her head out. 'Excuse me—Caz, is it? Will you come in here a moment please?'

Amaryllis thought Caz stiffened a little, but otherwise she did not move. The woman repeated her words in a louder voice and Caz turned slowly and made a 'who—me?' face.

The woman beckoned and Caz came over, reluctance in every step. 'Yes?' She sounded puzzled. 'Did you call me?'

'I certainly did,' said the woman with a smile. 'We have a little mystery and your friends seem to think you could help sort it out.'

Caz's blank gaze swung over the other girls, 'Oh, hi,' she said vaguely. 'Wendy—isn't it?' Barbara nodded nervously.

'Is this the one, Amy?' the woman asked Amaryllis. Amaryllis nodded.

'Well, perhaps you could explain about the book,' said the woman, looking at Caz. 'The book you asked Amy to get for you. How were you intending to pay for it? Have your parents an account here?'

Caz looked blank. 'I don't know what you're talking about!' she said.

'Amy here,' said the woman patiently, indicating

Amaryllis, 'said you asked her to get a book. This book.'
She tapped the parcel on the counter. 'But it seems you
didn't give her any money to pay for it. Well?'

Caz brought her shoulders up. 'Well what?' she said.

'Well, how were you intending to pay for the book?
It is for you, isn't it?'

Amaryllis nodded. Caz shook her head.

'We seem to have some difference of opinion here,'
said the woman drily. She turned to Katie. 'You. What
do you know about this?'

Katie shook her head again, turned and bolted out of
the shop. Barbara and the ginger girl followed. Sharon
looked at the woman scornfully. 'It's her,' she said
loudly, pointing to Amaryllis. 'She made it all up to get
us into trouble. Make it look as if we'd been nicking
things—she's always doing it.' Her voice trailed off as
Caz shot her a look of sheer venom.

'Well,' said the woman briskly. 'Perhaps it might be
best if we simply forget all about this sale and put the
book back on the shelf.' She looked thoughtfully at
Amaryllis. 'If I were you, I'd stick to doing my own
shopping, dear. And you—Caz—next time you want a
book you come in and buy it yourself.'

Caz's face flamed.

The woman continued to look at them sternly until
they trailed out of the door.

The other three were waiting sheepishly at the far side
of the mall.

'What the hell did youse go and run out on us for?'
blazed Sharon.

'Wasn't much good us waiting about to be caught,' said Barbara.

'You left us though. You left *Caz!*'

'So?' Barbara sounded defiant.

'So you don't get away with things like that!'

'Shut up,' said Caz quietly.

'How can you just stand there and . . .'

'I said, shut up! The question isn't whether Barb should have taken off at all. It's about Amy.' She turned to Amaryllis. 'Well, Amy? Do you feel like telling us why you did that?'

Amaryllis went cold. She had thought these girls would go away once their leader was humiliated. 'I did as you asked,' she said. 'I got you a book.'

'And then made such a song and dance about it the woman got the wind up. Why did you do that?'

'To make you look stupid, of course!' snorted Sharon.

Caz considered. 'Shall I tell you what I think?'

The others nodded sycophantically.

'I think Amy was trying to be clever. Trying to get us into trouble. I don't think Amy wants to be part of the gang any more—do you?'

The others glanced at one another uneasily.

'That's all right then,' said Caz briskly. 'She doesn't have to be our friend if she doesn't want to be! But that doesn't mean she can try to spoil things for everyone else. Let's give her a nice little going-away present to remember us by.'

Katie and Barbara looked at one another and backed away a little.

'What? Do you two want out as well?' asked Caz
pleasantly.

'N-no,' said Katie. 'What are you going to do?'

'Not me, Katie,' said Caz. 'You. It's what you're going
to do. Where's her bike?'

The others looked at one another. 'I don't think she
had it with her,' said Barbara.

'No,' agreed Sharon. 'She didn't. That's how we came
to leave ours behind at your place with Marina.'

'Marina?' Caz looked about. 'Oh, *Marina*. I thought
I hadn't seen her about. We'll have to think again then.
But not here.'

'Let's go to the park,' suggested Sharon with an
unpleasant grin. 'It's nice and quiet there.'

'No, I've got a better idea,' said Caz slowly. 'Amy's
going to throw a stone through the cop shop window.'

'Nah,' said Barbara. 'She'll never do that.'

'Of course she will!' said Caz. 'We'll all be witnesses!'

'But—don't we all have to stick together?' asked Katie
timidly. 'We can't dob on her.'

'The gang sticks together,' said Caz. 'But Amy isn't
a member of the gang any more. Remember?'

Amaryllis had never thought to be so frightened of
girls her own age. She cried out as they hustled her
along the paved walkway, but it didn't seem to help.
Several people looked up, but seeing a bunch of girls
passing by, they simply shrugged and went about their
business.

'Everything OK, kids?' asked one brisk-looking
woman.

'No!' cried Amaryllis, but the others hustled her on while Caz lingered to say something reassuring.

'What'd you tell her?' panted Sharon as they passed beyond the mall.

'Told her Amy'd just got dumped by her boyfriend,' said Caz briefly.

'What, Day with a boyfriend! That's a laugh!'

And all the time they were moving away from the grandam's house.

At last they slowed down and hustled her in behind a low hedge. Amaryllis found to her fury that she was shaking so much she could hardly stand and her breath was hurting her throat.

'It's just up there,' said the ginger girl, pointing across the road to a brick and concrete building.

'What is this place?' asked Amaryllis.

'Geez, Day, don't you know anything? This is the cop shop,' said Sharon with satisfaction. Bending suddenly she picked up a short brownish bottle from among the roots of the hedge and held it up in triumph. 'Just what the doctor ordered!' she said, tossing it from hand to hand.

'Give it to her, you dork,' said Barbara. 'It'll be covered with your fingerprints.'

'Oh, don't be a spazzbrain,' said Sharon. 'The cops don't take fingerprints from kids. If you're under fourteen or so they don't even take you to court mostly: just haul you up in front of the Inspector.'

'How do *you* know?' said Katie.

'Me cousin said. Now, how're we going to do this?'

'Give Amy the bottle,' said Caz gently. Her fine boned

face was pale, but burning red along her cheekbones.

Amaryllis dragged her hands behind her back and kicked out, catching the ginger girl on the knee.

'Cool it!' snapped Caz as the ginger girl staggered against the hedge and began to hop and howl. 'You want the cops out straight off?'

'Well she hurt me!'

'Take the bottle, Amy,' said Caz. 'Take it!'

Amaryllis kept her hands clenched, but Sharon handed the bottle to the ginger girl. She put both hands on Amaryllis' forearm and twisted vigorously in opposite directions.

Amaryllis gasped with the pain and tried to pull away.

'Open your hand,' panted Katie, appalled.

'Look—better stop or she'll be yelling next!' said Barbara.

'Of course we'll stop!' said Caz. 'As soon as she's done her little job.'

Amaryllis kicked out again. Something hit her in the side of the face, something else thumped her ribs and the hedge came abruptly against her cheek.

'Now!' said someone, and Barbara and the ginger girl laid hold of Amaryllis. Sharon took careful aim and flung the bottle over the hedge towards the window of the brick building.

It bounced off the frame and shattered on the foot-path. For a moment the girls stayed where they were, appalled. Then Katie gave a wail of fright and broke away.

'Don't run!' snapped Caz. 'Sharon—stop her!'

The blonde girl dived for Katie and hauled her back.

Then there were loud angry voices and running feet, and nobody was holding Amaryllis any more.

'Go on then!' said Sharon viciously, and gave Amaryllis such a shove that she staggered and fell out onto the footpath beyond the hedge.

# 25. AMY
## *Truth*

my opened her eyes and squinted painfully. Her eyelids hurt, which was no wonder since they seemed to be encrusted with salt. She rolled over and the rest of her began to hurt too, stinging and smarting and throbbing with underlying aches.

'Owwwww,' said Amy sadly. She felt black and blue and purple all over, but she was alive.

Her head spun as she heaved herself up on her elbow, and she looked ruefully down at the mess of sandy grease and draggled lemon-butter hair. It would take forever to get the knots out . . .

She was lying on a beach, but it certainly wasn't Bondi, nor anywhere like it. The sand was coarse, grey and gritty, the sea sucked noisily two metres away and she couldn't see Western Port anywhere.

What if she'd drowned and ended up in yet another world? She groaned. But perhaps after all she'd just come ashore in the next bay along. That current had been pretty awesome.

It would be a long walk back. And what if Lord Random and the creepess had already gone back to the island and missed her? Lord Random had said he wouldn't be back, but he wasn't exactly the most honest person in the world. Any world.

The sun was high, so she had been there quite long enough. Amy struggled the rest of the way up and squirmed out of her bundled-up mantle. It was probably ruined anyway.

Still, she couldn't wander about in drawers and a petticoat, so she laboriously worked open the knots and shook it out.

Sand flew and the blue cloth glinted bravely in the sun. No wonder reinbeast weave was so popular! thought Amy. If cold salt water and sand couldn't harm it, it must be pretty near indestructible!

Well, since she was alive and—for the present—free, she'd better head for Western Port, and get there before Lord Michael was arm-twisted into giving up the golden reinbeast. He'd be scouring the town by now in any case.

Unfortunately, heading for Western Port was going to be more difficult than it sounded, for the beach was a mere half moon of grey sand walled in by ferocious-looking cliffs. Amy sighed and put on the damp mantle. If she was going to be climbing, she'd need some protection for her legs and arms. She really felt more like sitting down and having a good moan, but there was no-one to hear her except for the wheeling birds and nowhere to go except up. Unless she fancied another swim.

She was resting on a ledge a painful ten metres above the beach when she heard voices and the regular dip and swish of oars. Her spirits seemed to descend to her shaking knees.

She'd never be able to outclamber Lord Random. She'd simply cling there like a fly on a window and wait to be swatted.

Like blazes she would!

Amy's fingers were aching and trembling with the strain of clutching the rock, but a scrambling sound below made her risk a glance over her shoulder. Just you try coming up here, Lord R, she thought, and I'll kick you off the cliff! Then she almost fell off the cliff herself as Amaryllis' spellhound bounded gracefully up beside her with a small whimper of delight.

'Red!' she gulped. 'Oh, Red!' His underparts were dripping with water, and Amy painfully removed one hand from the rock to stroke his ears. But then her joy at seeing him again—and apparently whole and unharmed—soured.

'I suppose you escaped from that horrible sewing dame and came to find me,' she said aloud. But if he had, might he not also have led the Tenth Castle kidnappers in her direction?

Fearfully, she looked beyond him, to the boat which was now nosing into the narrow crescent of the beach. Of course the oarsman was facing away from her, but to her unutterable relief, the person staring up from the bows was Crag.

The expression on his face was so ludicrous that Amy began to laugh weakly, a sound which sounded, even to her, suspiciously like sobbing. She put her spare arm around the spellhound's shoulders and hugged him close, fizzing and dripping and salty. For he had somehow escaped the Tenth Castle with his teeth undrawn, his sterling spirit undaunted and an army of rescue at his back. Well—almost an army.

Crag stumbled ashore and floundered up the beach without waiting for the other man to drag up the boat.

'Amaryllis! How are you here?' he cried. He sounded rather scandalised.

She looked down. 'Thank you very much for asking, Crag, I'm just fine,' she said with sarcasm. 'I'm bruised and sticky and all wet and I've been kidnapped and intimidated and half drowned and most of it's your fault.'

By now Crag had reached her. 'You fell over the cliffs?' he asked in astonishment.

'No,' said Amy. She giggled weakly again. Suddenly it seemed very funny indeed to be clinging to a cliff and answering silly questions. 'Look, let me come down. Down, Red!'

Crag insisted on helping her into the boat, where Red settled at her feet and began prosaically to lick his paws dry. 'You have the hound to thank for your rescue,' said Crag. 'The hound and Jarman.'

The boatman turned to smile at her and Amy recognised Sophie's seafaring sweetheart. 'Indeed, Miss Amaryllis, I did but guide the craft,' he said cheerfully. 'The Bright One did disallow knowledge of you, but at her word the spellhound did lead us to a cavehold in the cliffs. Those who live there professed to know naught, yet the hound would have its way. Your brother played the minstrel in an inn where we heard more of Lord Random's ambition than he might wish, aye, and saw a dame of his household most greviously dishevelled and raving of a maddened spellhound, and frowned at by the lord in consequence.'

'The isle!' spat Crag. 'He held you there. But we found the gown among the rocks and feared you dead. Jarman here is a man of the sea. He knows the currents here and we thought . . .'

Amy forced her bruised face into a smile. 'You reckoned you'd be sure to find me washed up on this beach!' she said. 'Well you were right—nearly.'

Crag nodded. 'We feared . . .'

'The Gullet is treacherous indeed,' put in Jarman.

'Grossissimo!' said Amy. 'You were looking for my corpse! Amaryllis' corpse I mean!' She knew she was babbling now, lightheaded with relief.

The boat began to toss uneasily as Jarman turned it into the waves. 'How . . .?' said Crag.

'I swam,' said Amy. 'And then I floated.' She pulled the reinbeast mantle across her chest and lifted her chin as Lady Jasmin might have done. 'You didn't think I'd let that creep get his hands on your father's reinbeast, did you?'

It was dark again when Amy finally met with the Bright One. Before that there was confusion and explanation, joyful tears from Sophie and the grimmest expression Amy had ever seen on Lord Michael's face. She loved him for it, for she knew Mike would have looked just the same if anyone had threatened his daughter.

'It seems I have been careless,' he said. 'I knew Random for a malcontent: I had not thought him like to sink so deep. And to make use of his lady mother so!'

'Maybe she made use of him,' suggested Amy, but in Lord Michael's world a lady was a lady and would have the benefit of his doubt. 'And Crag—' he said, 'what were you about to deal with such a man?'

'It wasn't his fault,' said Amy. 'I shouldn't have left the inn and I shouldn't have left Red. The Bright One told me not to.'

'The message he gave Amaryllis was not the one I sent,' said Crag.

'What need had you to send a message at all?' enquired Lord Michael.

The fat's in the fire now, thought Amy. Poor old Crag. She saw the boy take a deep breath.

'Last eve I played for Master Ash at an inn,' said Crag.

'Indeed?'

'He is willing to take me as apprentice.'

Lord Michael said nothing at all.

'Lord Father,' said Crag, with the air of one desperate to get it all off his chest, 'I would have gone with him at first light, had he been willing to take me without my lord father's consent. But he is an honourable man.'

'More honourable than my son it would seem!' said Lord Michael coolly. He turned away. 'Your deceit has almost caused the loss of your sister and her spellhound as well as of your heritage.'

'Lord Father . . .' said Crag, but Lord Michael brushed him away.

'Later,' he said. 'I will speak with this Master Ash and if he is as you say you may go to him. Perhaps he will teach you more than music, for it seems that I cannot.'

'He did come to save me,' said Amy. 'And he brought Red and Jarman. And I still have to see the Bright One. The real Bright One—Jadetha.'

'Indeed you must go on the morrow,' said Lord Michael. 'She must lay hands to soothe the hound and renew the charm on your birthchain. When it arrived broken at the inn . . .'

Amy shivered suddenly. 'Couldn't we go tonight?'

So at the end of that long uncomfortable day she did finally meet the Bright One in the deserted Bright Pavilion.

Lord Michael, Crag and the spellhound escorted her there and entered the pavilion with her, but the Bright One gestured the two men to stay back, and beckoned to Amy. 'And so we meet again, child of the castle, child of the crag,' she said in her lilting voice. 'And here is my dear hound as well.'

'Could you look at him, please?' said Amy. 'I think the sewing dame tried to do something bad to him. She sort of clapped her hands over his head and threw something . . .'

The Bright One made much of Red and said he'd taken no great harm from the sewing dame's attempts to maze him. 'The fool is naught but a mumblecharm, and not a well-taught one either,' she said. 'Indeed, 'tis likely the charm by which she sought to confuse the hound will by now have rebounded upon her.' She smiled at Amy with a malicious twinkle in her odd-coloured eyes. Facing the real Jadetha, Amy wondered how she could have been fooled by Lord Random's lady, even for a moment.

'I thought I met you yesterday,' she said. A shudder crawled up her back at the memory. 'Lord Random's lady. She was so like you, and she was wearing the same clothes.'

The woman sighed. 'We of the Seventh Castle have ever our renegades,' she said. 'We are not all born to the same skills, and the disappointed ones are seldom content with what they have. I had a close kin-sister among them, and perhaps she has taken the twisted path. Have you still the luckpiece I gave to you at our last meeting?'

'Yes, but it's gone all dull,' said Amy. She dug in her pouch for the coin, wincing as sore shoulder muscles protested. The token slipped from her bruised fingertips and fell to the stone floor, where it rang like silver.

'Perhaps you'd better have it back,' said Amy. 'It isn't really mine, you know. I mean, it isn't me you meant it for.'

The Bright One made no move to take the charm. 'I have something else you may have need of,' she said.

Amy nodded eagerly. 'The book,' she whispered. 'The green ledger!'

'Indeed.' The Bright One lifted the cover from her basket and lifted out the green leather book. 'This belonged in the beginning to one of the Seventh Castle,' she said. 'A bright lady who wed with a lord of the reinbeast emblem. She forswore the byways and lived with him in his castle: her wares she took to her new home, but I doubt she sold them ever. She was your great-grandam, if I am a judge, and through her blood you have the right to your brave companion here.' The spellhound laid his head on her lap.

'Not me,' muttered Amy. 'Not really. I don't have any rights at all.'

'What then will you give me for the ledger not truly your own, child of the crag?'

Amy raised her bruised face. 'I'll give you the truth,' she said.

Abruptly, the Bright One signalled to Lord Michael. 'My Lord, take the minstrel to his master at the inn,' she said. 'I'll mend and strengthen the maiden's birthchain and bring her safe home. On the morrow your daughter and her hound will return to you and you may carry them safe to your castle.'

Lord Michael looked a query at Amy, but she smiled at him and nodded. 'I will be safe with the Bright One, Lord Father.'

He looked doubtful, but bowed to the Bright One and turned to leave. 'Until the morrow, my Ryllis,' he said.

'Until tomorrow,' echoed Amy sadly. 'And . . . Crag?'

Crag turned to her. His face was strained, but he looked somehow less of the sulky boy he had been before. 'Ryllis?'

'Thank you for coming,' said Amy. 'I was never more glad to see anyone in my life than I was to see you and Red. And I hope the master teaches you to be the best minstrel in all of Ankoor.'

Crag gave her a brief smile and followed his father.

'And now,' said the Bright One, 'pay my price.'

So Amy sat beside the Bright One and wrapped herself warmly in the reinbeast mantle, dry now and seemingly undamaged by its immersion in the cold sea.

'You see,' she said, 'my name is really Amy Day . . .'

# 26. Amaryllis
## *Marina*

At that point two people arrived simultaneously from two different directions. One was a gangly young man in a blue uniform who dashed down the steps and across the street, turning to call over his shoulder to someone still inside the building. 'Bloody kids behind the hedge!'

The second was Craig Day, with the girl called Marina panting a long way behind him.

The young man in blue reached Amaryllis first. He bent and hoisted her to her feet then looked at her with a frown of amazement. She raised an uncertain hand and dabbed at her grazed cheek, then inspected the smear of blood on her fingers.

'What the devil have you been up to, Amy?' asked the man in blue. He handed her a handkerchief.

'I thank you,' said Amaryllis.

'Ammo!' yelled Craig.

'*And* Craig! That's all I bloody need!' said the young

man. 'Here, you look after her. I want to get a look at these others.' He crossed the street and peered over the hedge. 'And what do you lot think you're doing?' Amaryllis heard him say. 'Who chucked that bottle?'

'Oh, officer—isn't it awful?' said Caz's warm voice. 'We tried to stop her, really we did.'

'Stop who?' asked the man.

'Amy of course! Oops! I didn't really mean to say her name. Look, Amy won't get into trouble, will she? It was an accident. We were just mucking about and she said . . .'

'Just a moment!' The young man beckoned them out. 'I think all you lot had better come into the station and explain in there.'

'Oh, Amy! You didn't do that—did you?' It was Marina, the thin girl who had stayed behind to look after the bicycles.

'Of course she bloody didn't!' snapped Craig. 'Ame couldn't chuck a bottle that far to save her life! You all right, Ammo?'

Amaryllis opened her mouth, but her cheek hurt so she changed her mind and stood mutely holding the handkerchief over the graze.

Across the street Caz was still expostulating. Beside her, Sharon was nodding self-righteously and Barbara and the ginger girl were standing by supportively. Katie was in silent tears of terror.

'I did not throw the glass,' said Amaryllis to Marina.

Marina dropped her eyes. 'I didn't really think you would have,' she admitted. 'Who was it—Sharon?'

Amaryllis nodded.

'But they'll all get together and say you did it!' said Marina hopelessly. 'You know they will!'

'Geez, don't think much of your taste in mates, Scrawny,' said Craig.

'Don't you understand?' said Marina to Craig. 'They'll blame Amy. All of them! And the cops will believe them, not us!'

Craig chewed a fingernail. 'Don't reckon,' he said. 'Come on over.' He took Amaryllis' arm and crossed the road to tap the man in blue on the shoulder. 'Hey—Jon— got a minute? I think Marina's got something to say.'

The six of them were invited into the building where a fierce sergeant lectured them very sternly indeed for some time. 'Now I don't ever want to see any of you girls in here again!' he ended, and let them go.

Caz, suddenly diminished, went home without a word and the rest of the gang members melted away.

'Sorry about that, Cousin Amy,' said the young man in blue, rubbing his nose. 'Couldn't treat you any different from the others or the sarge would've had my guts for garters.'

Amaryllis understood at last that Craig and Amy were somehow kin to the law enforcer in blue. Certainly the grandam, when she arrived shortly afterwards, spoke to him as if to a familiar child. She then insisted on loading Craig, Amaryllis and Marina into her vehicle and driving them back to her house in Severne Crescent.

Amaryllis was restless that night. Her face hurt and so did her ribs. The stuff the witch—Gran—had put on her bruises seemed to have worn off, and so had the comfort she had had from the gran's assurances.

'Don't worry about it,' said the grandam's voice in her head. 'It'll all come out in the wash, so don't let it get to you.' But how could it fail to get to her? She wanted to go home.

She was in a troubled doze when the disturbance came: a thud and a muffled yell.

'Owwww! Blastissimo!' hissed a voice beside her ear. 'Now I've gone and cracked my head *again!*'

Amaryllis stiffened, and reaching out a cautious hand she touched something warm and solid and alive.

Whoever it was gasped and hit out. 'Hey, who's there?' it whispered fiercely. 'Don't say I've got somewhere else!'

Amaryllis shrank back against the wall, and then groped for the light switch, encountering another hand apparently doing the same thing.

The light snapped on, blinding her for an instant. When her eyes adjusted, she found that she was looking at herself.

'You're—you must be—' Her voice croaked, and she cleared her throat. 'You're Amy. The real one. But what have you done to your face?'

'Wowissimo!' breathed the other girl, staring. 'I suppose you're Amaryllis! But hang on, you look just like me! I thought you had . . .' Her voice trailed off as she put a hand to her head and touched one long plait. 'Oh no! I thought we'd just swap back over. If it worked at all. The Bright One didn't say anything about this!'

Amaryllis sat up slowly. The Bright One! She was one

of the Seventh Castle, surely, and not to be spoken of
lightly.

'How come you're still here?' said the other girl. 'Why
haven't you gone home again? And what have you done
to your—my—face?'

'Someone hit me,' said Amaryllis. 'I fell into a hedge.'

'Oh—oh! Don't tell me—is today the 13th? And you
met up with Caz? Geez, I'm sorry!'

Amaryllis nodded. 'She wished me to be a thief. I
would not, and I told the stallholder she should watch
her wares. Caz did not like this, and she wished for me
to break glass near the police station. Your friend
Marina—she helped me and so did Craig and a kinsman
called Jon. I am sorry if this Caz was your friend. She
is no longer.'

'I bet she isn't!' breathed Amy. 'But Marina stuck up
for you! Wowissimo! And—did you say—Craig? I *don't*
believe it!'

She scrambled out of the bed and settled her mantle
of reinbeast blue. 'But look, we've got to get you home
again. I mean to Western Port. That's where you'll wake
up, I think.'

'Western Port!' cried Amaryllis. 'I have never
been . . .'

'No, but I have.'

'And your face, what have you done to your face?'

Amy touched her bruised cheek gingerly. 'Well I sort
of went swimming. Lord Random shut me away on an
island and I had to get away somehow. It isn't just my
face, either. I'm lumps and bumps all over.' She sat on
the foot of the bed. 'Look, this is a long story. I'd better

tell it in order.' She launched into a long and involved narrative.

'So here I am,' she finished abruptly. 'But I can't see why you're still *here*, looking like me. I thought we'd just swap back. Perhaps you have to write in the book too. *My* book. You haven't lost it, have you?'

Amaryllis shook her head. 'I have no green book.'

'Blastissimo! I suppose Mum's been in here clearing up again. Have to ask her in the morning. Or you will! She'll think you're me. Gollissimo, we *are* alike, aren't we? Come over here.'

Amy tugged Amaryllis over to the mirror. Grey eyes mirrored met mirrored grey eyes and Amaryllis nodded.

'Except for our hair,' continued Amy, tugging energetically at one dangling plait. 'Ow. It's still sore. Sophie just about combed it off my head trying to get the knots out. Anyway, the Bright One will explain it all to you so you can understand. All you need to do to get back is find the green . . . Oh-oh!'

Amy's explanation broke off as the door began to creak open. Pushing Amaryllis back towards the bed, she crouched down and burrowed underneath.

'What's all the flamin' noise about?' asked Craig, slouching into the room.

# 27. Amy
## *Book*

ell?' demanded Craig.

Amy heard Amaryllis sit down on the bed.

'Hey, Amy! What's up? You were talking to yourself or something. You OK?'

Silence.

'Amy?'

'Yes, it was Amy. I was talking to Amy,' said Amaryllis.

'Blastissimo!' said Amy under her breath. She watched from beneath the trailing bedspread as Craig's large bare feet and the too-short bottoms of his pyjama legs came into view.

'Oh, not that again!' said Craig, but he sounded weary rather than cross. 'Look, Ame, I'd better go and get Mum. I know Gran said not to worry, but it's getting worse. Hell, you're even talking to yourself!'

Under the bed, Amy's eyes bugged. Could this really be horrible Craig? Worried! About *her*!

There was a creak. Craig was sitting on the end of the bed. 'Listen,' he was saying. 'You know you're really Amy Day, don't you? All this Amaryllis rubbish is just something you've dreamed up . . .'

This, decided Amy, had gone quite far enough. Though why the girl had been crazy enough to tell Craig, of all people, she couldn't imagine.

'You're a flamin' nuisance sometimes, Ame,' complained Craig's voice, 'but you *are* my sister.'

Wowissimo! What a cue! thought Amy, and she crawled out from under the bed.

'She's not your sister. I am,' she said. Or at least she started to say it, but unfortunately she put her knee down on the front of her mantle and tipped over on her nose. 'Blastissimo!' she exclaimed crossly. 'Another bruise!'

Craig gawked as Amy got herself untangled and stood up. He made a sort of disbelieving gargling sound in his throat and stared wildly from Amy to Amaryllis. He began to shake.

'Hey!' said Amy pleasantly. 'Don't look so pleased to see me!'

'No,' muttered Craig, staring at them. 'I don't believe it. I don't. I'm schizzo, that's all. Ame—Ammo . . .'

'I'M Amy, *she's* Amaryllis,' said Amy helpfully, 'I got stuck with the plaits in the transfer and I picked up the bruises getting away from Lord R. Now I suppose we'd better get you back home, Amaryllis, and hope the hair goes with you. I suppose we'll sort of swap bruises. Now where's that book?'

'N-not so fast!' stammered Craig.

'Look,' said Amy. 'Get out, Bro. We've got a lot to

do and there's no way Amaryllis can go home with you here distracting her.'

'She's not going anywhere until I find out what gives!' Craig barred the door.

'She's got to, numbskull! Since we're both here, neither of us is there, and just think how fussed Lord M will be if she doesn't turn up at the inn! And, besides, if I were you, Amaryllis, I wouldn't leave Red with the Bright One for too long. Her grandam knew his and he thinks she's wonderful.'

Amy turned her back on Craig and began scrabbling hopefully about the floor. 'C'mon, help me find that book! Green, with a gold pattern . . .'

While the girls searched and Craig sputtered, Amy hurriedly filled in a few more details about what had happened during her time at the castle. 'I hope you didn't like Lord Random, Amaryllis?' she said. 'He's in deep, but deep, trouble! Oh! And your father has got the most beautiful golden reinbeast baby!'

Amaryllis exclaimed with delight.

'And Crag has gone to be a minstrel, so I think if you play your cards properly you'll be your father's apprentice one day . . . Ah!' Amy pounced on the bookcase and drew out the green-covered book. She took a ballpoint from her desk, opened the book and handed it to Amaryllis. 'Well, go on—write! Write something about your own life. Go on! And you!' she said to Craig. 'What are *you* staring at? Go back to bed!'

To Amaryllis' utter amazement, Craig obeyed. She stared at her determined other self. (Had she *really* routed a lord of the Tenth Castle?) Then she sat down at the desk and began to write hesitantly. Her pen moved over the paper in a series of ornamental loops and flourishes, as approved by Master Greenhaven. It was one of the wonderful pens that never seemed to run dry.

Amy watched her for a while and then lay down on the bed. She could watch just as well from there, and really, her bruises were hurting a lot. She didn't think she'd ever want to swim in the sea again . . . She let her hand trail down by the bed, missing Red's strange/familiar presence. She frowned.

It seemed a bit hard that she should have moved Heaven and Earth (and quite a few other things) to get home to this life only to miss the one she had fled!

Suddenly she sat up. 'Where's Reg?' she asked.

Amaryllis looked up ruefully from her seat at the desk. 'The poor hound! Oh, how he hated me at the first! But he is a good creature and just lately he has almost been my friend.'

'Oh.' Amy tried not to feel chagrin. After all, she had been pretty thick with Amaryllis' dog. 'Amaryllis?' she said wistfully. 'I really wish you could stay a while so we could talk about everything. I mean—we ought to be friends, don't you think? We've been one another . . . And hey—I've had a great idea! Why shouldn't we . . .' She saw Amaryllis was still holding the pen. 'But I'm interrupting you, aren't I?' she said. 'I'll be quiet until you've finished writing, and then we can talk until we go to sleep. We can share the bed—after all we've shared everything else.'

She lay down again and closed her eyes, which stung still from the salt water.

# 28. AMY

## Sister

my opened her eyes to a dazzle of daylight. Ugh! She felt terrible. All sore and cramped. She put her hand uncertainly to her forehead,which was grooved from contact with the edge of the desk. She must have actually gone to sleep sitting up. Weirdissimo!

But hang on a minute. *She* had been lying on the bed. Amaryllis had been the one sitting at the desk.

Or had it been Amy at the desk and Amaryllis on the bed? Thinking about it made her head ache, and she rubbed crossly at her short spiky fringe. Ugh. Double ugh. Her hair felt all chewed off. Maybe she'd let it grow . . . now she'd got her own body back.

'Oh, no!' wailed Amy, hit by a sudden appalling sense of loss. 'She's gone and we didn't have our talk and I didn't get to tell her my idea.' But there seemed to be nothing she could do about it now.

She was ruefully checking out her bruises when someone tapped on the door. 'Yeah? What?' she called irritably. She had that home-from-a-holiday, just-finished-a-good-book feeling, and she wanted to be left in peace to come slowly down to earth.

Craig's face appeared warily around the jamb. 'It's me, Ame,' he said unnecessarily. His eyes darted around the sunny bedroom. 'Ame?'

Amy blinked at the brightness. What was Craig going to have to say this morning? 'What?' she said unhelpfully.

'I've got . . .'

Whatever he was going to say was drowned in a banging door, a sudden skidding of toenails on the short-piled carpet and a weird howl of canine thanksgiving as Reg burst into the room and hurled himself on Amy like a hurricane, knocking her over. He whined and sobbed and grovelled himself into her lap. Amy dodged a lick in the eye, put her arms round him and gave him a good hug. 'All right you old monster—get off now,' she panted. 'Ugh—what've you been eating? And what are *you* staring at?' she asked, catching Craig's mesmerised gaze.

Craig made a gulping sound. 'Ame? El Creepo? Want to come for a swim?'

'So long as it isn't in the sea,' said Amy, picking herself up from underneath Reg. Wasn't Craig going to say anything else? *Surely* Craig was going to say something else. Unless . . .

'That didn't put you off, the other day?' he mumbled.

'What?' said Amy.

'Nearly getting drown . . . hey, Ame, listen.'

Drowned? Drowned when?

'What are you on about?' she said. 'Siddown, Reg, you old monster.'

'Oh—nothing.' Craig shook his head and dug his hands into his pockets. 'Well, come on if you're coming, Scrawny.'

'Call me that, and die,' said Amy automatically. But suddenly she thought she saw what Craig was trying to do. He was testing her, as she had tested Crag Loveday on that first morning at breakfast . . .

And he was looking at her with doubt in his eyes. And he looked pale under his summer-time freckles. 'Schizzo,' he remarked.

Amy met his gaze. '*Are* you?'

'Aw, come on, Ame. Give us a break! How did you . . .?'

They looked at one another uneasily.

'There must be *some* way of proving it,' remarked Craig. His eyes swivelled around to Amy's desk, where the green-covered book lay open. Craig went into over-drive and reached it a second before Amy did, snatching it away to read the story, which began in his sister's large, rather uneven writing.

\*\*\*

*In a castle on a cliff above the great Sea of Storms in the land of Ankoor lived Amaryllis Loveday. Her father was Lord Michael, a very important person who loved Amaryllis so much that he gave her a priceless namegift, a spellhound named Red. As long as Red was with her, nothing could harm Amaryllis . . . not even Lord Michael's enemies, who were*

232

*jealous of his wealth and power. At the castle
Amaryllis had a very good friend . . .*

\*\*\*

'Give it here, you creep!' cried Amy, incensed. 'It's
mine!' And then, unable to stand the suspense . . .
'Well?'

Craig held her away with one hand and ran his eye
down the page to where the writing changed abruptly to
a fine elaborate script, ornamented with loops and
flourishes. Slowly, he lowered the book so she could see.

'That's her writing, isn't it?' he croaked. His colour
had faded another degree. 'Amaryllis? The girl who was
here last night. The one who's been here instead of you.'

Amy nodded slowly, and together they read what
Amaryllis had written.

\*\*\*

*After many adventures Amaryllis exchanged news
with her friend Amy Day, and then returned by night
to the abode of the Bright One, where she was
greeted by her spellhound and made secure. In the
morning she was transported to an inn at Western
Port where she greeted her lord father and found her
brother gone for a minstrel. This saddened Amaryllis,
for she had come to value her brother's society, yet
she felt that in the future all would be well . . .*

\*\*\*

'Ame . . .' said Craig, still in that strange hoarse voice.
'Ame, I nearly drowned her. I thought she was you,

233

mucking about, and I threw her in Jase's pool . . . She couldn't swim! She looked just like you, but she couldn't swim!'

'Well, it wasn't your fault. Geez, where she comes from, I couldn't even get dressed by myself!' said Amy. 'Lucky I had Sophie to help me or I'd've been up the creek and no mistake. Sophie was great, but she didn't really believe me.'

Craig sighed. 'Tell me what happened,' he said. 'The lot. There's got to be some logical explanation, some-where.'

'If I do,' countered Amy, 'will you believe me?'

'I don't know,' said Craig honestly. 'But I'll try.' And somehow that pleased her more than a glib assurance would have done.

'And hey, why didn't you tell me the run-in you were having with Caz Brandon? Nicking things from shops— hell! Real spazzbrain country!'

'I didn't think you'd care. Were you nicer to her than you are to me?' asked Amy, suddenly jealous.

Craig stared. 'Yeah, of course I was!' he said. '*She* wasn't my sister!'

Amy shivered. 'She could have been,' she said. 'If things had been different.'

'Look,' said Craig awkwardly. 'Don't you worry about Brandon. She's history. And if anyone gets after you again, let me know, eh?'

'Thanks,' said Amy, touched. 'But I guess if I can flim-flam Lord Random, I can handle anyone. You just wait till I tell you what a creep *he* is!'